The Darke Academy series:

1 Secret Lives

2 Blood Ties

3 Divided Souls

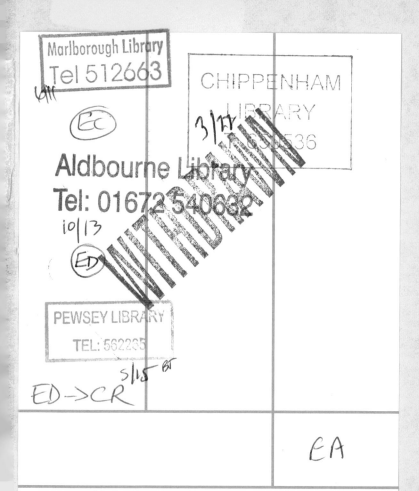

DARKE
ACADEMY
DIVIDED SOULS

GABRIELLA POOLE

Hodder
Children's
Books

A division of Hachette Children's Books

A Catalogue record for this book is available from the British Library

ISBN 978 0 340 98926 5

Typeset in Berkeley by Avon DataSet Ltd,
Bidford on Avon, Warwickshire

Printed in the UK by CPI Bookmarque, Croydon, CR0 4TD

The paper and board used in this paperback by Hodder Children's Books
are natural recyclable products made from wood grown in
sustainable forests. The manufacturing processes conform to the
environmental regulations of the country of origin.

Hodder Children's Books
a division of Hachette Children's Books
338 Euston Road, London NW1 3BH
An Hachette UK company
www.hachette.co.uk

PROLOGUE

This was no chore.

Yusuf Ahmed smiled down at the girl who sat on the velvet couch, far more in his hungry eyes than the prosaic lust of a boy for a girl. Touching her jaw with a finger, he drew a gentle line to her chin: tantalising himself and her, feeling the hunger grow and letting it.

'Another *raki*?' He proffered the carafe.

'I think I've had enough.' Her voice was teasing.

He gave a soft laugh. *Yes*, he thought. *Yes, I think you probably have.*

Yusuf took a small step away from her, enjoying the masochistic kick of prolonging the wait. He was hungry, but not so hungry he would rush it.

Raising his eyes to the open window and the balmy night, he let himself soak up the beauty of it: the moon on the Bosphorus; the lights of a cruise ship strung like a glittering diamond necklace. High and hazy in the warm evening, the dome and minarets of the Blue Mosque gleamed like chalcedony.

It reminded him vaguely of Sacre Coeur, of last autumn term in Paris, when everything had changed. When things had begun, for the first time in so very long, to go awry for the Few. When that scruffy waif of a scholarship girl, Cassie Bell, had turned up at the Academy and been shockingly chosen by Estelle Azzedine, then tricked into becoming the new host the old woman needed for her powerful spirit.

He wished now that he'd never got involved . . . though he still remembered with some relish the frisson of excitement at the joining ceremony, the sense of entitlement and arrogance and power. He vividly recalled the Bell girl's fury as they held her down at Estelle's mercy, and he recalled too the unexpected pity – and fear – he had felt in himself. Because it had gone wrong so fast. The joining ritual interrupted; part of Estelle's spirit joined with Cassie, part of it shut out in the void; and the Few left as stunned as if a bomb had gone off in their midst.

Yusuf shook his head. A new term had now begun, and the girl Cassie seemed to be settling into being one of the Few. He was actually glad. They were all glad. Or most of them were . . . So who knew what brighter turn things might take for the Few? Including himself.

Closing his eyes, he inhaled warm air scented with night flowers, sea breeze, petrol fumes and charcoal smoke. Gods, he was going to love it here. This was his final term at the Academy, and he felt a keen sense of regret mingled with the anticipation. His future glowed before him with wealth, success and influence: how could it be otherwise? But still, he'd miss the comradeship, the secrets, the power of being one of the Few at the Academy. It had been fun.

A light hand touched his arm. Yusuf turned to the girl, suddenly aching with the beauty of the night and with hungry longing.

She blinked. Her eyes were already a little unfocused and distant, her smile trembling on her lips as if she'd half forgotten it was there.

Good . . .

He set down his own glass and took her face between his hands. She was lovely, with her golden heart-shaped face and her huge dark eyes. Her lips parted and she made a small sound: it might have been desire or bewilderment, but he no longer cared. She'd drunk what he'd offered her. She wouldn't remember.

For one moment longer, he hesitated. Feeding like this

was forbidden, because it was too dangerous. But for that very reason the thrill made it irresistible. And Yusuf was nothing if not experienced. He was strong, he was skilled.

And *damn*, he was hungry.

Gripping her face, he brought her lips fiercely against his own. He felt the momentary simple pleasure of human contact. Then, inside his chest, the spirit pulsed and energy gushed into his veins. His eyes widened, reddening.

As the girl made a small moan of protest, he forced himself back under control. He wouldn't hurt her: that wasn't how he got his kicks. Relaxing his hold, he intensified the kiss, feeling life-energy thrill to his nerve-endings. Oh, this was feeding, this was satisfaction, this was *bliss*.

His senses sharpened, smell and taste suddenly acute. He could hear the thrum and beat of the city, the throb of the cruise ship's engines. He could hear a soft footstep. And then a whisper said his name.

Yusuf Ahmeeeed . . .

Had he misheard? Releasing the girl, he went still, listening intently.

He'd chosen his place well: this secluded room with its romantic arches and nooks, above the restaurant in Old Istanbul. He'd paid the owner *extremely* well because he'd made it perfectly clear he did *not* want to be disturbed.

How did they know his name? Was it someone who knew him from the Academy . . . ?

He shivered at the thought. That was trouble he didn't want, not right at the end of his school career. Unauthorised feeding, in a forbidden manner? It wasn't beyond possibility that he could be kicked out, like Katerina Svensson after the business with the Bell girl. Sir Alric took his rules very, very seriously . . .

Silent, every sense alert, he turned towards the darkness beyond the window arch. He stepped closer, then became preternaturally still as his eyes searched the night. Below him was a courtyard and the balcony extended round three sides of it, draped with shadows.

There. Against a cracked tile wall, one shadow darted past quickly.

Someone was spying on him. One who knew his name. Taunting *him*: a sixth former, one of the most powerful Few! The spirit inside him kindled, but this time with rage. How *dare* they!

He'd satisfied his hunger, and now the romantic moment was lost too: one more reason to turn his fury on the intruder. He touched the girl's face. Gradually, gently, she came back to herself, eyes focusing, mouth curving into a more determined smile. She trailed a hand down his chest seductively, her fingers hooking on his gold chain and rolling its shark tooth pendant between her fingertips.

'Aren't you going to kiss me, then?'

If only you knew, he thought dryly.

'Sorry, *habibi*. I've had a text, it's an emergency. You have to go.'

Her sulky pout was delicious to behold. He laughed. 'I'll see you tomorrow night. I'll make it up to you, yes?'

'Oh, yes. You certainly will.' She winked, blew him a tantalising kiss and was gone.

Yusuf gave one last yearning sigh, but his muscles were already tensing for a chase. Light and swift, he vaulted through the arch and out on to the rickety balcony. The dark figure had had plenty of time to make an escape, but only when he dropped lightly down to the courtyard did Yusuf see it break into a run. *Foolish*, he thought.

The figure managed to keep several steps ahead of him as they chased through the alleys of Sultanahmet; its footsteps were almost as deft and light as Yusuf's own. It was growing dark and lonely as they travelled through the streets, the sounds of the city muffled by distance, as if he had pursued the shadow into another time zone. No one around.

Slowing, he realised with surprise that the figure was

heading up the steps of an outbuilding beside the Hagia Sophia. Was it a mausoleum? Still, Yusuf felt no fear. He approached the entrance and realised the crypt was empty of people, closed for renovation. But as he entered, despite his expectations the place was not dark. Above him a domed Byzantine ceiling gleamed in the light of hundreds of candles.

Candles . . . ?

He stopped, ears pricked. Every inlaid door leading off the room was open.

Yusuf was very alert now. Beyond the vast atrium, the place was a maze of arches and passageways, and whoever the prowler was, he was hiding. And he was very good at it . . .

Yusuf felt himself thrill at this stealthy hunt. Not a wasted evening, really. An opponent was almost as much of a kick as a lover. He was going to teach this upstart a lesson.

Ha! Movement, sharp, at the corner of his eye. *There*, beyond that arch with its chipped and faded gilding. Yusuf moved, swift and silent as a cat.

The anteroom was small, with fretwork cloisters and half-destroyed blue mosaics, and the glow of candlelight didn't penetrate the shadows beyond the pillars. There was no exit: it was a trap. Yusuf halted, smiling wryly. Time to turn the tables and flush him out, this insolent stalker.

'Show yourself.' His voice, clear and commanding, echoed through archways.

In response there was only silence. He turned a slow half-circle, eyeing every corner, every shadow.

'There's nowhere to go. Face it.'

Still nothing. The flickering golden air was heavy with the stillness.

'Who the hell are you? Show yourself *now*.'

A movement, a sound behind him. It might only have been a footfall, but it was close. Too close.

He spun on his heel, tensed to strike, furious at the audacity. The glint of a smile met him, and another, more sinister glint.

'*You!* What the hell—'

Yusuf staggered back, flinging up his hands in horror. He didn't even have time to scream. Couldn't run. Couldn't shut his terrified eyes. He only felt, for the first and last time, a crushing and paralysing terror as the figure sprang for him.

Then every candle in the building went out and Yusuf's world turned to absolute blackness.

CHAPTER ONE

Three weeks earlier

'I miss him.'

Cassie Bell remained quiet. Her friend looked over at her again.

'Jake. I miss him.'

'I know, Isabella,' Cassie replied. How could she forget . . . ?

Seared by guilt, Cassie kept her eyes studiously fixed on the blue water and the bright morning over Istanbul. She had no right to get impatient with her lovelorn roommate. It was partly her fault, after all, that Isabella Caruso's beloved Jake wasn't coming back to school this term.

She wished Isabella could be happier, that was all. It wasn't just that she hated to see her friend so subdued;

she wanted to stop feeling so bad about it herself. There was a whole new term ahead, a whole new city to discover. And a whole new Cassie, if she could keep her focus and reboot her school life.

'Beautiful, isn't it?' She nudged the Argentinian girl and smiled, then nodded at the view.

With a visible effort, Isabella pulled herself together and focused on the blue Bosphorus and the city beyond the yacht's bow rail, all hazy domes and minarets. A slow smile curved her lips as if she couldn't help herself.

'Yes, you're right. It's stunning.'

Cassie had never seen a skyline quite like it – though that was hardly surprising, since she'd only begun to be introduced to the exotic cities of the world less than a year ago. Until then, her life had alternated between unsuccessful foster homes and Cranlake Crescent care home. Thank God *that* was all over.

Another shot of guilt. Cassie gulped and tightened her fingers on the rail. Cranlake Crescent wasn't exactly the Darke Academy, but it had been home for a very long time, and it hadn't *all* been bad. There had been her mates, and the younger kids who looked up to her – and, of course, there had been Patrick Malone. Her friend, her mentor, her key worker. Kind, supportive Patrick.

Patrick, who betrayed her by sending her to the

Darke Academy without bothering to mention its terrible secret . . .

She shook herself. Going over and over that shocking discovery from last term didn't help – finding out that Patrick had known about the dark spirits of the Academy, known that they inhabited some students and fed on others. He had *known* the danger he was sending her into. But still he'd sent her.

It was hard to forgive him but, despite all that had happened, over the holidays Cassie had been willing herself to do just that. He was her link to the past, the closest thing to family she'd ever known. She missed him, damn it. The problem was, she didn't know where to start. She'd cut him off dead last term, telling him that she never wanted to see him again. That was why she hadn't been able to return to Cranlake Crescent for the Easter holidays: she hadn't known if she could face seeing Patrick. So when Isabella had extended her holiday invitation, Cassie had nearly bitten her hand off.

Bitten the hand that fed her . . .

No. She'd *jumped at the chance*. That was a better way of putting it. And sailing the Mediterranean on board Isabella's father's luxury yacht, from one exotic ancient port to another, was certainly no penance. Still, seeing Isabella with her family, so close and loving, had pierced her in a vulnerable spot. She needed to reconcile with what passed for her own family, she realised. She needed Patrick.

Cassie tugged her phone from her pocket. Biting her lip, she scrolled down to his name. Go on, she thought. No time like the present. Just a quick text. Nothing too effusive . . .

Taking a deep breath, she thumbed a few buttons.

Hey. Howz it going?

She pressed send before she could think twice, then shoved the phone back in her pocket. After what felt like for ever, but was probably only about seven or eight minutes, it vibrated and bleeped. Nervously, she checked the reply.

From: Patrick Malone

Cassie. So happy to hear from u. Are you ok? We all miss u.

Cassie smiled sadly. She could tell he was still a little wary, and she wasn't surprised. She hadn't exactly given him much reason to hope she'd be in touch again any time soon. She quickly ran her fingers over the buttons.

I miss you guys too. Sorry I've been out of touch.

Another brief pause, then her phone vibrated again.

I understand. Cassie, cld I come 2 see u? No pressure, but I have a few days off due. Can I come out there?

She couldn't help her grin as she texted back.

Yes! I'd like that. Email me with details. X

God, it would be good to make up . . .

Cassie's grin was still in place as she glanced up towards the sun deck where Isabella's mother was already sunbathing, engrossed in a paperback. Although they weren't her family, the Carusos were the kindest, most generous people she could have hoped to meet. Well, they would be: Isabella must have got her nature from somewhere. Despite the stealth that was necessary so she could feed on Isabella – and she felt terrible about deceiving her friend's parents – Cassie had felt at home from day one, and she was going to miss them. She was going to miss the sea, and the long idle days, and the *Mistral Dancer* itself.

But still. *Istanbul!*

She didn't know where to look as she gazed towards the land looming towards them – at the fine villas and mosques and the little villages on the Asian shore, or at the magnificent domes and minarets against the blue European sky on the other side. She was almost tempted simply to dive off the boat and swim ashore, so eager was she to investigate the ancient city. And she *could* do it. She wasn't about to drown, not with the power of the spirit inside her, not now that she'd finally settled into a pattern of regular feedings over the holidays.

Thanks to Isabella, Cassie's spirit hadn't gone hungry. She had stopped trying to deny Estelle's needs, in contrast with her denial at the start of the previous term. Well, all except Estelle's biggest request – to allow the divided parts of her spirit to reunite inside Cassie, as they had done momentarily during that horrible night last term . . .

Cassie shook the memory free from her mind. She wasn't going to think about all that now. Things had finally settled down – even Estelle seemed to have accepted Cassie's adamant refusal to let her be 'whole'. For now at least, she seemed content with the way things were. With a surreptitious glance at Isabella, Cassie felt a surge of gratitude and affection. Where would she be without Isabella's generous offer, of her own free and spontaneous will, to be Cassie's life-source? It didn't bear thinking about.

And yet here was Isabella looking so miserable, lost without her Jake. Their passionate, fleeting romance had ended with Isabella's agreement to allow Cassie to feed on her against her boyfriend's understandably adamant wishes. How had the three friends ended up like this? Cassie thought she might burst into tears herself if she didn't lighten the mood. She exhaled deeply.

'So . . . Do you think the shopping's any good?' she said, smiling at her friend.

Isabella shook herself, pushing her windblown hair out of her face, the edges of her mouth turning up ever so slightly. 'Well, I have been thinking about it a little, I must admit. We could get the Grand Bazaar out of the way early, yes? Because we must be touristy for a little while.' Her smile broadened; she was making an effort, Cassie realised with a surge of affection. 'And then – the boutiques! The galleries! The wonderful designers!'

'The maths lessons . . .' Cassie wagged a finger at her, and they both giggled.

'Oh, those too, I suppose.' Isabella linked an arm through Cassie's. 'We'll try to make it good, won't we?'

'Course we will. We're going to have a brilliant term!'

'Yes. Even if it has to be without *him*.' A shadow of gloom crossed Isabella's face once more. 'Oh, Cassie, I'm sorry to be such a misery mutts. I can't help it.'

'Misery *guts*! And it's OK, really. Of course you miss him.' She nudged Isabella, trying once again to cheer her up. 'But Jake's safe, that's the main thing. Much safer than he'd be if he'd come back to school, especially in his frame of mind. Look at it this way – he's far less likely to get into trouble in New York, right? It'll give him a chance to get some perspective on this whole idea of revenge for his sister . . . And more time to miss you, eh?'

'Well, *that's* true.' Isabella gave a small smile, but her face soon fell again. 'If he's even thinking about me. But I'm worried, Cassie. I mean, he still has that strange Few knife, we're pretty sure of it, no? And I—'

'Sh!' Cassie tightened her grip on her friend's arm as she glanced nervously back towards the cockpit and saw Isabella's father approaching.

'Girls! You see the Academy? Over there!'

Señor Caruso came over and stood behind them, gesturing with his ever-present cigar – which Cassie had never seen him light – towards something directly in front of the *Dancer's* elegant bow. With one last glance at her friend, Cassie looked in the direction he was indicating.

She'd expected more warning, but she'd been too busy talking and ogling the two shores of Istanbul. Now a small island lay ahead of them, so close it seemed she could reach out and touch it. Already the boat's captain was slowing the *Dancer*, slewing it round to starboard, aligning it with a jetty where several smart launches were already moored in the sparkling water. Now that they were broadside to the island, Cassie could gaze up in awe at the building that would house the Darke Academy towering above them.

It looked ancient – far older than the Academy in Paris. Gilded carvings glittered in the morning sun, and the spires and cloisters and colonnades were intricately tiled with blue and gold mosaic accented in blood red. Cassie could see massive carved doors framed by a soaring gilded arch, and the whole thing was crowned with a huge gleaming dome. It seemed built to intimidate. What had it been: a sultan's palace? Even Señor Caruso looked impressed. He clamped his unlit cigar between his teeth and narrowed his eyes, staring up.

'I think you will have a good term here, ladies!'

'And Isabella, you will try *very* hard with your mathematics, won't you, *mija*?' Señora Caruso injected, winking at Cassie as she came to her husband's side. 'I'll miss you girls so much, both of you.'

Cassie smiled back, a little overawed as usual by the warmth as well as the sheer gorgeousness of the pair: she with her mane of dark bronze hair that was so like Isabella's, he with his lean, polo-player's physique and his glittering eyes. Boy, she thought, the god of genes really did smile on Isabella. Cassie's own beauty had been mightily amplified by her induction into the Few – one perk she couldn't complain about. Maybe this term she'd discover others. She was determined to find something positive about this whole experience . . .

Her roommate was already hugging her parents as the crew piled her expensive luggage – and Cassie's two shoddy cases – into the small launch boat. Isabella's misery over Jake seemed to be momentarily forgotten amongst the bustle and excitement of arriving at the school.

New school, new start, she thought again, and Cassie found herself looking forward to finally making her mark on the Darke Academy. Excitement rose in her as she and Isabella bade their farewells, and she her profuse thanks, with hugs all round. It seemed barely any time at all before the Carusos were waving from the yacht rail, and the launch carrying Cassie and Isabella was cutting a smooth path through the blue water to the jetty.

This island, that imposing ancient palace that was to be their school: it was all so different from what Cassie had experienced in her previous two terms at the Academy. Yet, as she and Isabella walked through walled gardens to a shaded colonnade, once more intricately tiled and gilded, Cassie recognised familiar things too. Surprisingly, she found she was glad of them. A small pool, dark and cool, its fountain splashing beads of water on to black orchids. In a niche to her left, the familiar statue of Achilles, still knocking hell out of Hector. And there were some features, too, that maybe Isabella didn't register but Cassie certainly did – twisting mythological creatures carved around a pillar; or the embossed symbol of elaborate intertwining lines on doorways that were much like the broken Few emblem burned into her own shoulder blade.

Yes, a lot was still the same. And she was keen to prove that her relationship with Isabella hadn't changed either from when they had first met on Cassie's arrival at the school all that time ago. Despite everything, Cassie was determined that they could hold on to their friendship, and surely nothing could change it. Surely.

Cassie shivered when she tried to imagine how she'd have coped without her best friend. Isabella was an anchor when so much else was different.

Jake was gone. They'd been all for one and one for all – supposedly – but Isabella's new role in Cassie's life had been a step too far for him, especially after discovering the Few's role in his sister's death in Cambodia a couple of years back. But it was neither Isabella's nor Cassie's fault the way things had turned out. If he'd been a true friend, he wouldn't have abandoned them. He wouldn't have left Isabella, left the Darke Academy, hell bent on avenging Jess, at the expense of his relationship with poor Isabella and his friendship with Cassie. And yet they hadn't heard a word from him since. Who knew what he was up to now?

Guilt twisted Cassie's stomach again. Isabella had waited so long for Jake to fall in love with her, but as soon as he did, Cassie had, deliberately or not, managed to come between them. If the shoe had been on the other foot, Cassie had often wondered in the weeks since, would she have sacrificed love for friendship? She was almost certain she would have done the same for Isabella. Almost.

Yet there were times when her heart, her whole *body* still ached for Ranjit Singh. That couldn't be helped. But Cassie's own love life hadn't been any more of a success than Isabella's had turned out to be. It was over between Cassie and Ranjit – and her new start meant starting again without him. Estelle insisted they could live without him too; the vicious spirit that part-possessed Cassie was all for making it on their own. Ranjit had betrayed Cassie, after all. Betrayed them both . . .

Absolutely, Cassandra, my dear! We must forge ahead.

Halting in the passageway, Cassie stiffened. Isabella came to a halt a few steps later, and turned back quizzically.

Well, well, Cassie thought acerbically. There you are, Estelle. Back just in time to see your old pals, eh?

The spirit had been so quiet over the holidays,

apparently just happy and satisfied with her regular and lively food source. Trust the old bat to reappear in time for school term.

Tut tut, Cassandra! That's not a nice thing to call your old friend now, is it?

Cassie couldn't help a wry grin playing on her lips.

'Cassie? Are you OK?'

'I'm fine, Isabella. Sorry.' Cassie walked on to her friend's side.

'We're here. Look!' Isabella pointed to the wall beside a heavy carved door. There it was: the familiar plaque.

Cassandra Bell

Isabella Caruso

Cassie released one of her battered cases and placed a hand against the warm old wood of the door. She cocked an eyebrow at Isabella.

'Shall we take a look? Or shall we just go for a coffee and not bother?'

Isabella laughed. Turning a huge iron ring, she swung the door wide.

Cassie was silent for a moment, breath caught in her throat, as Isabella marched into the room and dumped her bag.

'Well,' sighed Cassie at last. 'The interior décor just gets better and better . . .'

She was gazing across a huge room, filled with ornate mahogany furniture, colourful rugs and tapestries, *kilims* strewn across sofas. Directly facing her was an arched window, the shutters flung open to reveal lush gardens, and beyond them the shining Bosphorus and the city itself.

Isabella had already flung herself on to one of the four-poster beds, pulling the drapes around her like a cloak. She peeked out, covering the bottom half of her face as if she was a harem seductress. Still investigating, Cassie ignored her and pushed open another carved door.

'Holy herrings! The hand basin's solid marble.' Cassie gasped and pretended to stumble dramatically. 'And the bath too!'

'What about the loo?'

'Nah. Bog-standard ceramic.'

'How disappointing,' Isabella said with a small smile, as she flung away the heavy drape. 'At least it feels very different from New York here, huh? Not too many reminders of last term. I like it.'

'Mmm.' Cassie paused, trying to inject a brightness into the proceedings. 'Well, you're used to this kind of elaborate surrounding. Imagine how much *I* like it.' Standing at the window, Cassie stretched out her arms and inhaled the salty scented breeze. 'You'll soon be feeling cheerier, I promise you. You're sounding better already,' she said, glancing back hopefully at her friend.

'Mm-hmm.' Isabella didn't look at her, she noticed, but went on gazing up at the heavy silk canopy. 'I just wish . . .'

Damn it, Cassie, don't push your luck! Snatching up one of the *kilims*, Cassie threw it over her roommate, so that Isabella squawked and had to struggle free.

'Come on, hon.' Catching Isabella as she emerged from the tumble of fabric, Cassie smiled. 'It's rough, but we *are* going to have a good time here. You've still got *me*, right?'

Isabella rubbed one eye, and gave her a grin that was a little forced, but better than nothing. 'Yes, I still have you. And you will know better than anyone how I try to kick-start a good time, Cassie Bell . . .'

CHAPTER TWO

Shopping. She should have guessed. It really was kind of touristy, thought Cassie, but at least a light of sorts was back in Isabella's eye.

Beneath its elegantly arched and tiled roof, the Grand Bazaar was a tumble of noise and exotic scents: tobacco smoke, roasting nuts, spices. She'd lost count of the shops selling jewellery and carpets and Iznik pottery. The prices were outrageous, and Cassie wasn't about to buy anything except the pistachios they were nibbling as they walked, but Isabella was doing her best to get back to normal, and for her that meant retail therapy.

Brightening, Isabella strode into a shop and began to bargain over an especially beautiful *kilim*. She could have afforded it at the tourist price, of course, but Cassie had a feeling she'd want to haggle for the sheer sport of it – or usually she would. On this occasion

Isabella's heart just wasn't in it. After five minutes, with a shrug, the shopkeeper gave up on her. Cassie was beginning to feel seriously terrible about her friend's depressed mood.

All my fault, she thought. All my fault . . .

Pausing in the tumult to flick desultorily through a rack of colourful scarves, Isabella pushed her bag of pistachios into Cassie's hand with a sigh.

'You finish these. I'm not hungry.'

'Isabella, you haven't eaten all morning!'

'I'm fine. I'm just not hungry.' As if to reassure her, Isabella squeezed her arm and winked. 'And you always need feeding up.'

Inside her head Cassie heard a disgusted *harrumph*.

She must keep her strength up for us, my dear. She's very selfish . . .

'Shut up, Estelle,' she muttered.

Isabella gave her a look in which alarm and concern were equally mingled, but she didn't have time to question Cassie. Behind her someone shrieked over the shouts and chatter of the market.

'Isabella! *Cassie!*'

Cassie turned towards the direction of the excited voice, and caught sight of a hand waving beyond a knot of German tourists. A familiar face appeared then disappeared, bouncing up once more to get a clear line of vision, and Cassie grinned.

'Ayeesha, hey! Cormac!'

The Barbadian girl and the Irish boy wriggled through the crowds, managing not to disengage their hands. Still an item then, Cassie thought. She felt an unexpected twinge of envy: that could have been her and Ranjit, if he'd had the courage to fight for her. Annoyed, she shook off the thought. This wasn't about Ranjit Singh. New start . . .

'Hey, guys! It's so good to see you.' She accepted a hug from Cormac, and then hugged Ayeesha as Cormac seized Isabella and embraced her warmly.

Ayeesha gave her a brilliant grin, flicking her long braids over her shoulder. 'And good to see you too, Cassie. Looking *good*, girl! You've been feeding properly!' The Bajan girl drew back and wagged a mocking finger. 'About time!'

'Um. Yeah.' Cassie smiled awkwardly, trying not to meet Isabella's eyes.

Ayeesha dropped Cormac's hand to link one arm through Cassie's and one through Isabella's. 'Come and have coffee, huh? There's a few of us over in that little café round the corner,' she said, her soft lilt quickening with excitement.

'A *Few* of us, you mean?' asked Cassie dryly.

Cormac laughed. 'Sure, but you'll keep us all in check. And if you won't, I'm sure Isabella here will. Come on, girls!'

Cassie, to her surprise, found she didn't need any further encouragement. The elite Few weren't all her type, not by any means, but there were some of them she'd be very pleased to see again. And she understood them better, now that she understood their motivations, their comradeship, and their unnatural hunger that had to be fed. She was, after all, one of them – or at least part of her was.

As Ayeesha led them to the coffee shop, Cassie found herself looking almost eagerly for familiar faces. Mikhail wasn't there, thank goodness. Neither was the horrible Sara who'd tipped off the evil Katerina and her mother to Cassie's movements last term, nearly getting her, Isabella and Jake killed in the process.

But Vassily and Yusuf were sitting together gossiping, and India and Hamid waved as she approached. In the flurry of air-kisses, whether they were sincere or not, Cassie found herself relaxing, smiling. She couldn't help sensing the new-found respect in their greetings – and she was genuinely glad to see some of them, she thought. Oh, the irony. In fact, considering how she'd first felt about the Few, she was shocked at how at ease she was. It was almost as if she'd missed them.

Voluntarily or not, she realised this was kind of where she belonged now. So maybe Ranjit had been right. Maybe if she'd embraced being part-Few sooner, they would still be together? Maybe—

No. She didn't want to think about him. Definitely not now. Cassie shook her head to clear it, then smiled and returned Vassily's formal handshake. Out of the corner of her eye, she saw someone else turn and rise to his feet. A good-looking, rakish figure with a distinctly louche air . . .

'Richard. Hey.'

She'd tried to sound a little reticent, but the smile had dawned on her face before she could stop it. Tentatively, almost as if he was afraid of her reaction, the English boy returned it, but without much trace of his usual carefree arrogance.

Cassie swiftly dampened her smile. New attitude or no new attitude, some things never change. Despite Richard's constant pleas for forgiveness last term, and the invaluable information he gave which led Cassie to finding Jake before he was thrown into the Living Soil, there was one thing she could never quite get over. Richard had been the one to trick her into hosting

Estelle's spirit. She wasn't sure she could ever forgive him for that, no matter how much things had moved on since that fateful evening. Tightening her lips as she leaned forward to greet him, she avoided making contact with his cheek.

'Cassie.' He gave her a wary smile. 'Great to see you.'

'Yeah. You too.'

He greeted Isabella fondly, but he kept his distance from Cassie as they all sat down, their voices jumbling, eager to gossip and swap impressions of the new Academy.

'What do you make of the courtyard? They finally got the hang of having the statues outside!'

'Too right – but have you seen Sir Alric's glasshouse? Has to have a special place for his precious bloody orchids, eh!'

'I'm more worried about the food. I mean, there's going to be something other than cheese and olives, right?'

'Cormac, baby, don't you think of anything other than your stomach?' Ayeesha patted her boyfriend's trim midriff teasingly. 'So anyway, apparently there's going to be a huge emphasis on history and archaeology this year. Extra classes.' She rolled her eyes exaggeratedly.

'Are you serious? Ancient ruins and dusty digs? No thank you.'

'It could be fun!'

'Yeah, right!'

During the mêlée of voices, more than once Cassie found her gaze drifting towards Richard. To her surprise, he seemed to be concentrating on cheering up Isabella; her detached, gloomy look gradually faded as he joked and chatted. Watching him, Cassie felt a surge of reluctant admiration.

Admiration for his thoughtfulness, that was all. Not affection.

She told herself that she wouldn't fall for his charm again. So far, he was acting pretty meek around her, but that was as it should be; he *should* feel awkward. OK, so he was being sweet to Isabella right now, but that didn't cost him anything. Sweetness and charm were weapons to him, as far as Cassie was concerned. He was the one who tried to play all sides against the middle, even sucking up to the vile Katerina and her minions when it had suited him.

But it was hard to keep her resentment bubbling. Ever since she'd perceived Richard's spirit, Cassie had begun to understand him a little better, in spite of herself. His seemed one of the weakest of all the ancient and immortal Few spirits that had merged with their human hosts, so it was maybe no wonder that he played the game so carefully. Again she glanced in his direction. Again, he kept his eyes and his smile averted, wary of her gaze.

Cassie felt another tiny flicker of a softening towards him. Try as she might, she wasn't as mad at him as she'd expected. Maybe she'd been wrong – maybe her new attitude *would* allow her to move on, as far as Richard was concerned. Maybe she wanted to.

'When did you guys get here?' asked Cormac.

Cassie glanced at Isabella, but she stayed silent. 'Just this morning. We, uh . . . we came on Isabella's father's yacht.'

'Nice! That was a beautiful-looking boat.' Vassily was smiling at *her*, though, with only a brief glance at Isabella, which made Cassie a little uncomfortable.

Again she looked at Isabella, trying to draw her in. 'Isabella's parents are incredible. It was really kind of them to let me come along. I'm sure my friend here didn't give them much of a choice.'

Isabella gave a small chuckle and smiled at Cassie, but didn't inject anything further into the conversation. Cassie sighed.

'Hey, you're one of us now, or near enough,' Hamid said, laughing. 'You need to get used to this lifestyle.'

'Yeah, I . . .' Cassie smiled, with another glance at Isabella. 'I'm not quite there yet, I don't think, as I'm sure Isabella would tell you.'

Isabella smiled, and finally opened her mouth to respond, but the conversation had moved on again. Ayeesha set down her tiny cup of thick coffee dramatically, goggling at it.

'Man, this gets you going in the mornin'. I'll be buzzing all day!'

'And all night, with any luck,' added Cormac.

'Hmm, you might not want to press that Irish luck though, sweetie, or Ayeesha could well get tired of you,' India interjected with a grin.

The Few hooted with laughter, even Ayeesha, though she squeezed Cormac's arm affectionately. Cassie found herself joining in, but noticed uneasily that Isabella's laughter was forced and half-hearted. She looked as though she was starting to feel pretty left out.

God, Cassie really just wanted Isabella to be happy again. If she could just move past everything that had happened with Jake, then maybe things might be OK – but right now Cassie really couldn't see that happening. Funny how, when she'd first arrived at the Academy, Isabella had tried for so long to make Cassie feel happy there, and now here they were with their roles reversed. Because she was really getting there, Cassie realised with an inward smile. She was feeling more settled, she was starting to feel at home. As though she *did* belong.

That's my girl! That's my girl, Cassandra! It's about time we started establishing ourselves here . . .

Even Estelle's aside couldn't dampen her mood. Cassie laughed out loud again, slightly out of place, earning a quizzical look from Richard. And yet when she turned to him, he was focused on Isabella once again, arm resting nonchalantly on the back of her chair.

'Well, I don't know about you guys but I *love* it here!' exclaimed India. 'What an amazing place for my last term! I think I might go and take a look at the Hagia Sophia this afternoon. Who fancies it?'

'Wish I could,' said Yusuf with a wink, tucking his gaudy shark tooth pendant back into his shirt. 'I'm meeting someone.'

'Aren't you always?' Ayeesha pointed out, to more chortling.

'Well, I don't remember him ever trying it on with me,' said Richard, faux-hurt. 'What am I, chopped liver?'

Yusuf chuckled wryly.

'Maybe he just has better taste,' Cassie added, though she couldn't stop the smile on her face from softening the blow.

Richard shrugged and nudged Isabella. 'A little harsh,

your friend, isn't she?' he joked, though the twinkle was missing from his eyes. Cassie tried to ignore it, which wasn't hard as she then heard India chime up again.

'Speaking of hot dates, Isabella! When's that hunky Yank Jake Johnson arriving?'

Damn. India was only trying to include her at last, thought Cassie as her heart sank to her boots. But as they all looked expectantly at Isabella, the Argentinian girl's tan skin blanched.

'Um . . . I'm . . . I don't know . . .' Isabella looked desperately at Cassie, then down at her watch. She gave a weak laugh. 'Actually, I'm so silly. I forgot, I'm expecting a call from . . . from my mother. I had better be getting back. Nice to see you guys.'

She stood up so fast she almost knocked her chair over. Richard caught it and steadied it. Vassily, Yusuf and Richard stood up awkwardly but politely as Isabella began hurriedly gathering up her bag and jacket. Cassie rose to follow.

'Can I walk you girls back, then?' asked Richard, but Isabella was already at the door to the café.

'No. No, it's fine. You stay. Just a phone call. I promised I'd, uh, let her know how we're settling in. Bye!' Isabella waved quickly, and then ducked speedily through the low wood-framed exit.

'What?' Cassie heard India say. 'Did I say something wrong?'

'I think you just put your size six Louboutins in it, sweetheart.' That was Richard – but Cassie was already out of the door as well, hurrying to catch up with her roommate.

'Wait, Isabella! I'll come with you!' Cassie called, catching up and linking her arm through her friend's. She was relieved not to have lost Isabella in the thronging crowds.

'Sorry, Cassie,' said Isabella miserably. She sounded on the verge of tears. 'You were enjoying yourself. I didn't mean—'

'Don't be daft. It's cool, I was getting a bit bored in there anyway,' Cassie replied with a grin.

'Me too.' Footsteps slowed close behind them, and then Richard fell into step. 'Thought you might need a big strong man to protect you from the hordes out here.'

Cassie glanced at him in mild surprise, but couldn't help returning his ironic smile. 'Yeah,' she replied. 'Do you know where we might find one?'

'That is so sweet of you, Richard. I'm sorry,' Isabella sniffed, ignoring their banter and walking fast.

'Stop apologising, you silly cow,' said Richard cheerfully, his loping stride easily keeping pace with her.

'And hey, bella Isabella . . . I'm really sorry about Jake not coming back. What a prize *arse*, eh? And I'm not just talking about those tight glutes of his. You're far too lovely for him, and I always said so. If you're looking for a means by which to achieve some comfort . . .' He trailed off, raising his eyebrows suggestively.

Cassie half expected Isabella to stop in her tracks and slap him, but she only giggled and wiped her nose. 'Uh, I'll let you know. Thank you, Richard.'

'But of course,' he said, though his eyes kept flicking towards Cassie, as though he were checking her reaction. Cassie frowned. What did she care if he flirted with Isabella? Anyway, he was only doing it to make their friend feel better, right?

Even beyond the Bazaar the streets were hot and noisy, and already the calls to prayer were floating above the chatter and thrum of the city. Richard kept up a stream of chatter as they headed for the port – pointing out landmarks, tossing out morsels of history, making off-colour jokes. By the time they reached the waterside, Isabella was just about cheery enough to wave to the boatman and call out without a wobble in her voice.

As they began to board, Cassie caught Richard's arm, gesturing for him to hang back beside her for a moment.

'Listen, thanks, Richard,' she began. 'Really. I

appreciate it. She needed cheering up.' Cassie nodded towards Isabella ahead of them.

'No problem.' He cleared his throat awkwardly. 'I meant it, anyway. Jake *is* an arse.'

'He's got reason, Richard,' Cassie reminded him darkly.

'I know. And I'm sorry his sister di— was killed,' he corrected himself. 'But he doesn't have to take it out on Isabella. She's nuts about him, poor thing. Sometimes it's hard to get over someone, no matter how much has happened between you.' He muttered the last sentence, so Cassie wasn't sure she heard correctly.

'I agree with you about Jake,' she sighed. 'But I reckon the whole situation with those two is more than half my fault, so it's kind of hard for me to discuss it with her.'

Glancing once again at Isabella, who was chatting amiably to the boatman who had helped her aboard, Richard lowered his voice. 'And are you OK, Cassie?'

It seemed like that question was so loaded it could sink the launch. 'I'm fine,' she said stiffly.

'Really? I hope so, Cassie, I honestly do.' He swept a lock of hair out of his face. Following it with her eyes, Cassie was irritated at realising she found the mannerism attractive. 'Because while we're talking fault,' he continued, 'I suppose I've got a lot to feel guilty about myself.'

Cassie took a deep breath. He was leading, but now was as good a time as any. 'True. But listen – I've been meaning to say thanks for that as well, Richard,' she muttered quickly. 'For last term? You telling me where to find Jake that night, at the Puppet Theatre? I'd never have thought of that. If it hadn't been for you, he probably would have been dead before we even got to him.'

'Yeah, well there are many things I regret in life.' He winked.

'Seriously. For all we've said about him, I am grateful. And of course, so's Isabella.'

'Even though you two nearly got killed yourselves?'

'But we didn't. That was a good thing you did, Richard.' And more than Ranjit bloody Singh managed, she thought bitterly.

'I owed you that much, didn't I?' He made a rueful face.

She laughed dryly. 'Yeah. I guess.'

Very lightly, he touched her arm, then dropped his hand. 'And look, Cassie, I know I was a pain last term, asking you to forgive me all the time, but I promise not to give you a hard time any more. OK? I'll leave you alone now. On my honour.'

'Richard, that's not—'

'Yeah, I know. My honour's not worth that much.'

Not what I was trying to say, she thought, smiling with

a touch of regret. But he was already grinning and striding towards the boat where Isabella was waving from the stern.

Inferior, Estelle's voice injected. *Inferior stuff, my dear. He won't get us anywhere.*

Ignoring her, Cassie jumped down into the launch after Richard. As he began chatting easily with the young boatman, exchanging opinions about some dreary football match, Cassie went to Isabella's side.

'God, Cassie, did I overreact? I've just got to stop thinking about him,' Isabella announced fiercely, eyes on the horizon as the sea breeze tangled her mahogany hair.

Cassie hesitated. 'Well yeah, I think you might be right. Though I understand, babe. I really do.'

Isabella paused, and then spoke again. 'And *you* need to do the same, you know.'

'Huh?'

'Maybe I'm wrong, Cassie. But somewhere deep down, aren't you still thinking about Ranjit?' Isabella watched her with concern.

'No.'

Cassie's cheekbones reddened as Isabella raised an eyebrow.

'OK. Well I hope not. Seriously,' Isabella said, winding her fingers into Cassie's and squeezed them. 'Because that would just be a fine thing, wouldn't it? Staying in one of the most exciting cities on earth, and *both* of us pining for a pair of deadbeats who don't even deserve us? No. Tell you what, Cassie, I promise I'm going to try and snap out of it. I'm going to be like you. Single and ready to tingle.'

Cassie burst into laughter. 'Mingle!'

Isabella grinned. 'Deliberate mistake.'

'Freudian slip, more like!' Cassie found herself giggling with her roommate. 'Deadbeats who don't deserve us, eh? So Richard's got to you!'

'I think he's getting to you, too.' Isabella gave her one of her lethal rib-nudges.

Cassie gasped and laughed. 'As if!'

'Whatever you say, Cassie Bell. Still, perhaps you should let him . . .' Isabella turned haughtily away, but a small smirk was playing on her lips.

Cassie frowned at the island as it drew closer. She hadn't been thinking about Richard, and she sure as hell hadn't been thinking about Ranjit. *Hadn't.* Except to be angry, no, *furious* at him. Other than that, she couldn't bear to think about the boy. Mustn't. She couldn't deal with thoughts of his betrayal, his cowardice; not right now.

A small chuckle interrupted her thoughts.

It's all right, dearest. I'll take care of things for both of us!

CHAPTER THREE

'Feel your clay, ladies and gentlemen! *Feel* what it wants to be!'

Signor Poldino was full of the joys of early summer, bouncing excitedly on his heels. Did the man never run out of energy? wondered Cassie. The light that poured in at the open windows of the elegant room had a green tinge from the lush gardens, and she could catch glimpses of bright sky, but if she had to be in a classroom, this was one of the better ones.

She was aware of stifled giggles behind her – the sculpture class was barely containing its collective hilarity at whatever Richard was working on, but the arts master didn't seem to have noticed. Cassie, for her part, made every effort not to turn around and catch Richard's eye. Off to her right, Cormac was studiously forming an out-of-proportion pair of legs. He seemed to be taking it unusually seriously till he quipped out of the corner of his mouth, 'Feet of clay, Cassie.'

'Har har,' she whispered back sarcastically.

'You know what my clay feels like?' hissed Isabella, examining her piece as she stood next to Cassie. 'It feels like crawling under the table and dying. Look at this thing. It's *terrible!*'

And it really was unidentifiably awful. Cassie shrugged.

'I don't know,' she replied. 'I thought it might have been a Rodin pastiche!' She started to laugh, but it died on her lips. It was as if a black veil had been thrown over her, closing her off from the rest of the class, and out of nowhere, Cassie's light mood vanished.

The feeling in her chest was dark and intense and . . . yearning. Something was calling to her, tugging on her like a magnet. Cassie lifted her head and looked back, though she knew exactly whom she would see.

Ranjit.

A jolt of electric lust raced through her body, and she had to suppress an involuntary shudder of excitement. Where had he come from? How long had he been there? She certainly hadn't noticed him being there at the start of the class, and in fact she hadn't seen him at all around the Academy in the couple of days before the start of term. Not that she'd been looking, of course. Cassie had assumed he was off being dark and mysterious or doing Sir Alric Darke's bidding, which was usually his default position around this school.

But here he was now, tall and beautiful, his amber eyes boring into her soul, and she couldn't look away. He gave her a single hesitant nod. There was something indefinable in his expression: hope, and longing, and fear, all mixed up into one desperate silent cry. It was a cry that got an answer from deep inside her:

No! No! He rejected us, Cassandra! It doesn't matter if we want him. We're strong without him. More than strong enough just us, together!

Cassie swallowed hard and forced herself to tear her eyes off him and concentrate on her work. She didn't need Estelle for a cheerleader. Of course she was strong enough. It was nothing more than a minor infuriation that he still made her nerve-endings crackle and her heart crash against her ribcage.

Yes, my dear girl! More than strong, we're better than him! You and me! TOGETHER!

'For God's sake!' she hissed out loud. Blushing as surprised faces turned to her, she muttered, 'Can't get this to work.'

'I know the feeling,' mumbled Isabella crossly, jabbing

a forefinger into the mess of her sculpture. Then she looked up and followed Cassie's gaze as she glanced once again at the handsome face behind her. Isabella's own face darkened, and she touched Cassie's arm, smearing it with wet clay. Lowering her voice, she said, 'Ah. Cassie, are you OK?'

Cassie blinked. Was she that obvious? 'I'm fine. Fine.'

'Are you sure?'

'Yes! Stop it. I'm fine,' said Cassie, raising her voice more than she intended. She flushed as more students turned to look at her, and as she saw Isabella's hurt expression.

'Look, I'm sorry, Isabella,' she whispered. 'I just— You're right, it's a bit weird. Let's talk about it later, eh?'

Isabella nodded and turned back to her clay with a sigh. Feeling another stare, Cassie flicked her gaze towards Richard. He seemed very solemn, till she caught his eye. Then he winked, and smiled proudly down at his creation.

Cassie followed his gaze, and a moment later flung her hands to her mouth to stifle her explosion of laughter. She just about managed to disguise it as a coughing fit, and Signor Poldino hurried across to pat her back and reassure himself that his favourite student wasn't about to expire. As he fussed, Cassie turned back to

Richard with a deadly look. His eyes opened wide, innocent, and he splayed his hands questioningly above his suggestive sculpture. This might look like a fine pair of taut buttocks, his pleading eyes seemed to say, but that's only your dirty mind. To prove it, he slapped his hands on to them, closing his eyes briefly, then opening them and grinning.

'You,' she mouthed through her smile, 'are disgusting!'

It only made his grin all the wider.

Grudgingly, Cassie couldn't help but think that she was glad Richard was in class that morning. She couldn't deny that he'd cheered her right back up, and she wasn't sure she would have lasted the class without his lewd mischief-making to distract her. Not with Ranjit's lethal, beautiful eyes boring into her back. As soon as they'd cleared up and the class was dismissed, Cassie bolted. She wasn't going to hang about and risk a grisly confrontation with her ex.

Her *ex*. Yes, that was all he was. Cassie gritted her teeth and dodged swiftly through the corridor crowds, ignoring the wrench of misery in her gut. The spirit's gloating voice wasn't really helping; that only served to remind Cassie of how strong the pull of him had been, for Estelle as well as herself. Frankly, she thought, Estelle was protesting too much. But how might she expect a vicious spirit to behave when it was scorned and rejected? No wonder the old bat was bitter. No wonder she wanted herself and Cassie to triumph alone. If only Estelle didn't keep reminding her of his attractions.

Who cares about a pretty face? Hypnotic eyes? Hah! The feel of his skin? What's that worth? We thought he was our protector, didn't we? Our forever lover, the missing part of us. But he let you down, Cassandra! He betrayed you! Betrayed us!

Well, supposedly it was for our own good, Estelle, Cassie thought – though she could hardly believe she was using Ranjit's own defence as justification. Apparently he had to obey Sir Alric's orders to keep me out of the Confine . . .

He's a coward!

That he certainly is, thought Cassie grimly. She needed to keep remembering that. Ranjit could have tried, found a way around it. He had given up. Estelle was right. He had let her down.

For the rest of the day Cassie managed to avoid Ranjit. Maybe that was because she was so hyper-aware of his presence, but she was pleased with herself anyway, for pulling herself out of his magnetic field every time she felt the tug. Isabella seemed to realise she was having a hard time, because she stuck close to Cassie all day, taking her arm as they hurried away from each class. Of course, thought Cassie, her friend knew just how she felt . . .

'Go on, give me the gossip,' Cassie said in the lull between English lit and Russian. 'I bet you've picked some up already.' And besides shopping, a good gossip had always helped cheer Isabella up. Maybe it would work for both of them.

Isabella brightened a little, seeming glad to be distracted from her gloom. 'OK. Well, Alice,' she whispered, nodding across the courtyard at the English girl who'd once been the evil Keiko's roommate. 'Her and Yusuf, apparently, though probably not for long, knowing him. But they were in the boathouse last night. Richard spotted them kissing.'

'No!' Cassie stared at the girl. 'I thought Yusuf only went for other Few. I hope he's behaving himself.'

Isabella rolled her eyes. 'I don't think he's that picky. And of course he isn't, he's completely – what's the word? – incorrigible.'

'That isn't what I meant.' Cassie gave her roommate a meaningful look.

'Oh! Oh, I see. Well, I'm sure he's careful, even if it's – you know – *feeding* he's after. He's OK, really. Much nicer than Keiko.'

'Well, if he is, he better not let Sir Alric find out, with his precious rules. And anyway, you're so obvious, Isabella! You reckon he's *OK*? What, just because his eyes are the colour of eighty per cent Belgian chocolate . . .'

Isabella wiggled her eyebrows. 'You noticed that too, then!'

'Heh! What do you expect? He's Few – being pretty is part of the package,' Cassie grinned, though with a hint of sourness. Then again, maybe Isabella should do a bit of flirting, even if it was with the notorious Yusuf. So long as that was all it was, Cassie thought warily. Still, the girl certainly could do with a bit of fun. She seemed to be obsessing less about Jake – hadn't mentioned him since, oh, the lunch break – but when her friend was off guard, there was still that intense sadness in her dark eyes.

'How have you been getting on, Isabella? I know it's hard being back in classes and stuff.'

'Don't worry about me. I'm all right. Really.' Her smile was a little bit too bright, and Cassie ached for her roommate. Poor Isabella. Cassie had to start finding more ways to cheer the girl up; she owed it to her.

'Listen, if you really want to know what happened in the boathouse, why not go and have a little chat? He's right over there, and he keeps smiling at you.' Cassie jerked a thumb in Yusuf's direction.

'Oh, I don't know, I . . .'

'I can't believe you're passing up a juicy bit of gossip! Go on! And to be honest, I wouldn't mind knowing myself,' lied Cassie, 'but I'd never have the nerve to ask. He'll spill to you though. Give it a go.'

'He'll tell me *where* to go. And how to get there quickest.'

Cassie made her best puppy-dog eyes at her friend, and Isabella gave a small smile. 'OK, fine. I suppose it can't hurt to exercise a couple of flirty muscles, even if they are mainly in retirement at the moment.' Isabella seemed to pull herself together, with a hint of an old glint of mischief in her eye. 'Let me see how much I can get out of him. Coming?'

'You go ahead, scandal queen.' Cassie grinned, delighted at her success. Isabella would never take the philandering Yusuf seriously, but a bit of his attention would be bound to boost her confidence. 'You better report back to me, and I mean *everything*. I'm going to check my emails, see if Patrick's sent his travel details through yet.'

Cassie watched Isabella till she was sure she was chatting to Yusuf, then turned happily and headed upstairs.

Big mistake. Turning beneath the archway that led to their room, she came to a dead halt. An all-too-familiar figure was leaning against the door. Her heart lurched and she almost stumbled, and that made her even angrier. How could he still keep having this overwhelming effect, even now?

'What are you doing here?'

Ranjit Singh pushed himself upright, rubbed his neck. 'Waiting for you. Obviously.' He risked a smile.

Cassie didn't return it. 'I don't see why. We've got nothing to say to each other.'

'Don't be like that, Cassie—'

'Like what? I'm doing as I was told, aren't I? Doing what you want. Being a good girl.' She felt her face twist into a sneer. 'I mean, you made your position pretty clear last term, Ranjit, didn't you? We can't be anything to each other, we can't be together. It's not appropriate, it's not possible, it's not *allowed*.'

'Cassie, that's not what I—'

She shook her head violently, afraid she might lash out – or worse, burst into tears. 'We can't even stand by one another in a crisis, can we, Ranjit? Or at least one of us couldn't. So there's nothing to talk about.'

He opened his mouth, but seemed momentarily stricken. With a sound of disgust, she tried to shove past him, but he caught her arm in a fierce grip.

'Don't touch me!' she shouted, though something

inside her thrilled at his touch. He let her go as if her flesh burned him.

'I'm not here to cause trouble.'

'So why are you wasting your time? There can't be any other reason.' Even as she said it she could feel the closeness of him, the way she yearned to touch him, the almost irresistible desire to kiss him, draw him in, *consume* him.

'You still feel it,' he whispered.

Cassie opened her mouth to lie, but thought better of it.

'Yes,' she said fiercely. 'But it doesn't matter what I feel, never did. It's over, Ranjit. Get it through your thick head, and your spirit's too.'

Wrenching the iron handle, she shoved through the door and tried to slam it in his face. His beautiful face.

'Please, Cassie. Hear me out!' His eyes were brilliant with something beyond desperation as he gripped the door, holding it open. Excitement? Was that excitement she saw?

She hesitated, trembling – with rage, and with something else a lot less welcome. She exhaled until she had no more air in her lungs, concerned she might unleash the mysterious, invisible power that her unfinished Few ceremony meant she possessed; the power that had caused so much trouble last term. Then she spoke quietly.

'Go on, then. Say whatever it is you have to say. And then just – get out of here.'

He took a deep breath, dropping his arms to his side but wedging a foot in the door just in case she changed her mind. 'Cassie, listen. I've thought about it over and over, what happened last term. I've thought of nothing else.'

'Good,' she told him viciously. He ignored that.

'We meant something to each other, Cassie. You were *everything* to me. I've never felt anything like that, and I think – I know – you felt the same. Thought I'd get over it, but I didn't. I stopped even wanting to!' He raised a hand as Cassie began to protest. '*Please* hear me out! Look, I hate what I did last term. You were right. I should have fought for us. It was the biggest mistake of my life, Cassie, the biggest mistake *of my life*.'

'That's all very—' Cassie began, but Ranjit took a step forward, as if to seize her, only controlling himself at the last moment.

'I don't care what Sir Alric says. And I don't give a damn about the Council of Elders either . . .' He paused.

'What are you—'

'I love you. I love you, Cassie.'

Cassie froze. OK, the boy knew how to get her attention.

'What?'

'Listen to me. I love you. I have done since the moment I laid eyes on you. And it's not about our bloody spirits.' Cassie heard Estelle protest faintly in the background of her spinning mind. Ranjit continued. 'The fact that we're Few – or part Few – that's all irrelevant. I don't care what's between our spirits. I love *you*.'

She must have looked like a gobsmacked fish, but as his eyes bored inside her soul Cassie couldn't think of anything to say. How could she? He'd never said anything *like* it when he had the proper chance. He'd never said all of that when he could have. When it would have mattered, when they were together . . .

Ranjit leaned a little towards her, smiling wryly. 'I'm glad I finally shut you up.'

She shook her head violently, as much to clear her brain as to reject him. 'Ranjit – no.' She spoke through clenched teeth. 'It's no good. It's too late. We can't be together, *you said so*. And you tell me now you don't care about Sir Alric, but look what happened. As soon as he clicked his fingers, you let me down. You left me alone, Ranjit! You left me alone to face the Elders, and I've never been so scared in my life.'

Damn, damn. Her eyes stung, and she hadn't wanted that to happen. It made her angry. So angry, in fact, that there was suddenly more than a tear in her eye. Her vision was reddening, reddening . . . No. She blinked back the fury. He wouldn't make her lose control. Never again.

'I know I let you down, Cassie, and believe me, I've never stopped tormenting myself.' His voice was so beautiful, so intense. And his golden eyes were tinged with redness, too. Not anger, though: passion. 'I *will* make that up to you. I'll make amends for what I did, Cassie. I've found a way.' He stepped back from her, clenching his fists. 'I've found a way for us to be together.'

'Oh, you have? That's a turnaround since—'

'Sh!' He put a finger against her lips, and the electric shock of his touch shut her up once more. She stepped back to a safer distance.

'What do you want, Ranjit?'

'I want us to be together.' He smiled, his eyes intense. 'I've found something that's going to solve our problem. I just need a little more time.'

Cassie let out a short laugh at that. 'Of course. I knew it. Well, Ranjit, I'll believe that when I see it. And when pigs fly over the Bosphorus.'

He ignored her. 'Listen, Cassie. I'll leave you alone

for now . . . But just one more thing – the Knife. Do you have it?'

'The—'

'The Knife! I know you took it from Keiko and I—'

'What? No. I had dropped it in Central Park after . . . after the fight with Katerina and her mother. I'm pretty sure Jake has it now.' As soon as it was out of her mouth, she wished she hadn't said it, but she folded her arms defiantly.

'Jake?' Ranjit's face darkened and he frowned, but then he bit his lip and nodded to himself.

'Yes, Jake. Why?' she said.

Ranjit shook his head. Meeting Cassie's eyes once more, he smiled broadly. 'Never mind. We'll be together. I promise you that.'

He turned on his heel.

Cassie couldn't say a word. Her throat was clogged with rage, and disbelief, and unbearable desire, and she could barely even breathe. She could only watch as he walked away, boots clicking on ancient tiles, as he moved beneath the archway and vanished from sight.

CHAPTER FOUR

'THIS BUILDING IS AN ANCIENT MONUMENT!'

Isabella screamed above the music from the open doorway, hands clamped over her ears, but Cassie ignored her. Sure, the Bose sound system was cranked up to full volume, but she didn't care. She needed to blast Ranjit-bloody-Singh *right* out of her system.

'THIS WING IS SIX HUNDRED YEARS OLD, YOU VANDAL!'

'WHAT'S THAT GOT TO DO WITH ANYTHING?' Cassie yelled back, annoyed.

'THE VIBRATIONS WILL DAMAGE THE MOSAIC TILES IF YOU CARRY ON! TURN THAT DOWN!'

Isabella stormed across to the stereo, making a dramatic show of battling the sound waves, and clicked the mute. The silence that fell was like a wet blanket.

Cassie scowled. 'Spoilsport.'

Scowling right back, Isabella tilted her head to one side, banging her ear as if to loosen music that was lodged in it. 'And now, you can tell me what's wrong. I was right, wasn't I? You're pining!'

'Trust me, I'm not!'

'Cassie Bell, nobody plays that kind of music unless they are slitting their wrists over some boy, even if they are ready to kill him to boot! Out with it, girl!' Isabella plonked down on to the bed beside her. Cassie sighed.

'Ranjit *bloody* Singh—'

'I happen to know,' said Isabella primly, 'that that is *not* his middle name. However much you wish to make it so.'

Cassie sighed. 'Ranjit, then. Ranjit!'

'What has he done now? Or do you just need him here to punch? Shall I go and fetch him?'

'You don't have to,' spat Cassie. 'You just missed him, as it happens.'

Isabella's mouth gaped, then stretched into a grin. 'He came to see you?'

'Yeah,' Cassie said angrily. 'Like I haven't got better things to do than listen to him make excuses.'

'Oh, Cassie.' Isabella put an arm round her shoulder and practically squeezed the breath out of her. 'This is *good*! This means he is sorry, this means he regrets what he did!'

'What he *didn't* do,' Cassie corrected her bitterly.

'Yes, yes, I know. But he *did* come to see you! At least he's here, wanting to be with you, wanting to make amends. Not like . . .' Her face fell for a moment, and she gave Cassie an imploring look. 'You can't give him a chance?'

No, thought Cassie, though with another pang of guilt for her friend's misery. Ranjit was worse than Jake, much worse. Jake had his sister's death at the hands of the Few to contend with, not to mention the fact that his girlfriend was being fed on by one of them. Ranjit's excuses paled in comparison.

'How many chances does he need?' Cassie exclaimed. 'As far as I'm concerned, Isabella, he's run out. How could I *ever* trust him? Tell me that! When I was summoned to see the Elders, it was— I was terrified! He knew that! He promised to be there with me, and he knew how important it was to me. And he *didn't show up!*' Cassie bit hard on her lip, feeling the pain of the betrayal all over again.

'Cassie,' soothed Isabella. 'You told me he had his reasons. That Sir Alric would have voted you into the Confine if he'd shown up. Ranjit had to do what Sir Alric told him to do. You know that.'

Cassie shook her head firmly. 'No. He could have at

least got word to me. He could have found a way around it all. I've had a long time to think it over. All over the holidays, when, by the way, he didn't bother to get in touch with me. Not so much as a bloody text!' She drew a hand down her face, feeling the dangerous heat in her eyes again, breathing deeply to calm herself. 'Sure, he had his excuses for what he did. But he can always get his way, if he really tries! If he *wants* to.'

'Cassie, you can't say he didn't want to—'

'Well he can't have wanted it very much. Except now, all of a sudden, apparently he's got the magic solution. Well it's too late.'

'What?' Isabella said, blinking in surprise.

'Yeah. He says he'll find a way for us to be together! Right, sure. *Now* he decides he's made a mistake, so now he can find a solution. How convenient! Well, you know what? It doesn't suit *me*, not any more. He had his chance to fight for this relationship. As far as I'm concerned, Ranjit's all mouth. All talk, no action. And I can't stand that. I'm done with him.'

Cassie stopped, catching her breath. She was annoyed that she was getting so angry about Ranjit, and his ridiculous, mysterious plans. What was all that about the Knife, anyway? It was on the tip of her tongue to mention it to Isabella, but something held her back. She didn't want to bring Jake up again, especially not in relation to the strange, jade-hilted Few Knife. Oh, to hell with the Knife and to hell with Ranjit, Cassie thought. He was taking up space in her head again, and that was the last thing she wanted.

Isabella leaned back on her hands, watching Cassie thoughtfully. 'Well. Maybe you're right.'

'I know I'm right,' Cassie replied dully.

'OK. So it's time to move on!'

'What d'you mean?' Cassie gave her roommate a wary look as Isabella stood up and began to count on her fingers.

'Yusuf? No, he is all right but he's a rake and a scoundrel. Vassily? Mm, he's quite a nice one, Cassie. He has a very fetching – what do you call it? Arse? I think it's all that gymnastics. Or there's Perry Hutton . . . ?'

Cassie lurched forward, pretending to gag. 'Besides, I highly doubt I'm his type,' she said pointedly.

'That's true,' Isabella agreed, giggling. 'OK. Not Perry! Let me see: Bjorn Madsen? Michael Leaming? Jiri, Daniel, Kristofer? I'm running out here . . .'

'Mmm, sooner the better,' laughed Cassie. 'Give me a break!'

'Hang on. I've got it!' Isabella paused and gave her a sly look. 'Richard Halton-Jones!'

Cassie flung a pillow at her. 'Get lost! No *way*!'

'No . . . ?' Isabella nibbled her lip and eyed her closely. 'I thought you were getting a little bit fond of him again. Just a little? He did used to like you very much. Remember how into you he was in your first term?'

'Are you joking? Do I need to remind you where that led? Out of the question! Next?'

'Hm. OK. I still think you protest a little too much . . . But fine, then I'm stuck.' Her roommate pouted prettily.

'Good! Anyway, enough about me. When are *you* going to snap out of it and hit on somebody?'

As soon as she saw the look in her friend's eyes, Cassie regretted it. Isabella forced a laugh, but she could barely get her mouth to curve the right way. 'You are right, Cassie. I shouldn't make light of it. If *I'm* not ready, then maybe it's not fair to think you would be.'

'Don't be daft, babe. You were just being funny! Damn. I'm sorry, Isabella, I shouldn't have said anything.'

You idiot, she berated herself. Bad enough being responsible for their break-up in the first place: now you have to take the mickey out of the poor girl? It *was* different for Isabella.

For a start, Cassie was over Ranjit. Well, the rational part of her definitely was, in any case. Whereas Isabella wasn't even *starting* to get over Jake. And Isabella hadn't broken up Ranjit and Cassie; they'd managed that fine all by themselves. Isabella's romance with Jake, on the other hand, had been sacrificed to Cassie's new life amongst the Few. For Cassie's needs. For Cassie's sake. She didn't have any right to compare their situations; it was her who'd *caused* Isabella's.

'I'm really, really sorry. Truly.'

'No, Cassie, it's OK,' Isabella said, squeezing her friend's hand. With a visible effort, she brightened and knelt down by the stereo. 'We'll put the music back on, yes? Exorcise the pair of them!'

'Not a bad idea,' muttered Cassie.

'Good!' Isabella got up and bounced on to her bed as music exploded into the room again.

'UGH, CHANGE IT! THIS GUY'S *TERRIBLE*!' screamed Cassie. 'I'M NOT IN THE MOOD FOR DISCO DANCING!'

Isabella grabbed her arm and dragged her up, trampolining, limbs flailing, forcing Cassie to join in or be bounced off the bed.

'OH, YOU WILL BE!'

Hell, if you couldn't beat 'em . . . and Isabella was right. Why should they be miserable for the sake of two feckless boys? It was good to see her friend smiling, in any case. Laughing, Cassie bounced on her backside, then back up again. They were shrieking and laughing to outdo the music when Cassie heard another voice. It seemed no decibel level could drown this one out.

Yes, my dear, laugh! We've nothing to be sad about! We're going to conquer the world, Cassandra, just you and me. We don't need him, we don't need anyone else! Laugh!

CHAPTER FIVE

Ranjit really had thrown a spanner in the works of her head. It was almost twenty-four hours later, and Cassie was still feeling a bit put out about his declarations. She had to get back on track, rededicate herself to Project New Cassie, New Attitude. Leaning over the marble basin in her bathroom, she filled it to the brim with cold water and dunked her head in. Gasping with the chill, she forced herself to submerge her face completely. She *would* get him out of her mind, even if she had to wash him out.

From under water she heard her familiar ringtone, and groaning, she flung up her head in a shower of droplets.

'Hello?' she yelped. The phone was slippery in her wet hand, and she almost dropped it, then grabbed it and pressed it to her ear again.

'Cassie? It's me, Patrick.'

She gasped. 'Patrick! You're here!'

'Yes.' He sounded worried for a moment, as though despite their conversations and Cassie's agreeing for him to come, she may have changed her mind. 'You didn't forget my plane came in today . . . ?' he said, attempting a quick laugh.

'No! No, of course I didn't forget,' Cassie lied. And that was one more thing to blame Ranjit for, she thought grimly. 'I was just, uh, washing my hair.'

'Great. Well, that means you'll be fit to be seen at least, eh? Come and have dinner with me this evening? Meet you here at the hotel?'

'I dunno.' She grinned widely. 'Hmm. How much are you willing to spend?'

'I'm willing to spend a fiver, maybe.'

'Wow, the whole year's salary, eh?' she said with a laugh.

'Ha ha,' Patrick replied sarcastically, though she could hear his smile as he relaxed. 'It's really good to hear your voice, Cassie. I can't wait to see you. I mean, presuming that was a yes, right?'

Cassie chuckled again. 'See you at seven?'

'Hey, Cassie.' He opened his arms and grinned.

'Who are you again?' Cassie furrowed her brow, then smiled back and hugged him fiercely. 'I missed you. God knows why, since I've no idea who you are, but I did.' She was surprised at just how good it was to see Patrick again at last, and she felt nervous butterflies mixed with a warm, relieved glow.

The hotel was quite sleek and modern, and could have been anywhere in the world. It was a bit soulless, but who cared? Patrick was there, with his brilliant blue eyes and the laughter lines crinkling around them, just like always. He'd made an effort to smarten up, and his blue shirt actually had a collar, but he still looked as if he was religiously opposed to ironing.

'Listen,' she said, suddenly self-conscious again. 'Before we go in, I just wanted to say, uh, I'm sorry for cutting you off for a while there.' She gave him a rueful look.

'Oh, God, don't apologise. It was my fault, Cassie.' He hugged her again. 'I had no idea that . . . that all this would happen to you. You know that, right?'

She walked alongside him to the restaurant, keeping her arm linked through his. 'I know. I was still a bit pissed off with you, though. Couldn't help it.'

'It's OK. You were right to be angry.' He rubbed his forehead wearily. 'I knew what the Academy was about, but I was promised that no scholarship kid ever became Few. Nobody ever had. It was such a strict rule, I could never have imagined . . .'

'Hmm. Scholarships aren't supposed to be Few. They're often "food", though. Didn't you think I might end up as a life-source?'

'Yes, maybe.' Guiltily he rubbed a hand across his face. 'But I had such a good experience with my roommate Erik when I was at the Academy. He was honest, straightforward, no deception. I was happy to help him and he never abused my trust. I suppose I was naive; I suppose I thought it was always like that.'

'Yeah.' She let the maître d' draw out a chair for her, and sat down opposite Patrick, watching his hands as he nervously smoothed the white linen tablecloth.

'I thought it was worth it,' he continued. 'I thought, for the educational advantage you'd be getting, coming from your background—'

'I know, honestly. And you know what?' She quirked an eyebrow at him. 'I appreciate what you did. It's been a wonderful experience. I mean *everything* – the ravenous hunger for life-energy, the spirit I've got hanging about to chat to now, the supernatural fights . . .' She smiled at him. 'It's been fabulous.'

He remained solemn as he watched her eyes, then caught hers twinkling. 'Oh. That's a little Cassie Bell sarcasm, isn't it?'

'Yes,' she said contritely. 'Hey, it's been . . . different. But in a weird way it hasn't been terrible. I'm getting used to it all.'

He leaned forward, touched her hand. 'Are you sure, Cassie? Are you sure you're OK?'

'Sure. Really. I'm moving on, Patrick. New start. I'm Few' – or half-Few, she added silently to herself – 'and I'll live with it. It's not so bad. I'm controlling the hunger, it isn't hard, and Isabella is as understanding as I'm sure you must have been to Erik.'

'You're lucky to have such a good roommate.' He looked up at her over his menu. 'I was so happy when I heard that, Cassie. It makes a difference. I think she's a real rock, Isabella, isn't she?'

'I don't know what I'd do without her,' said Cassie truthfully. She laid down her menu and traced patterns on it with her finger. 'I bet Erik appreciated you too. Do you . . . do you still miss him?'

'All the time.' Patrick smiled with half his mouth. 'Erik was an amazing person. Even all these years later, it's hard to believe he's gone.'

Cassie clasped her hands and looked at him directly. 'What happened to him? When I asked Sir Alric about it last term, he wouldn't really go into details.'

Patrick took a breath and sat back in his chair. 'It was nearly twenty years ago now. In our final term. The

Academy was in Mexico City, and we had all these special classes and field trips in archaeology. It was a bit like here in Istanbul, actually. Anyway, Erik was working on a project with Sir Alric; they'd gone off to the Yucatán for a week. I remember how excited Erik was, how pleased he was that Sir Alric had chosen him out of all the Few students, trusted him. And he was fascinated by the project too, whatever it was.'

'You never found out?'

'Sir Alric came back alone on the third day. I knew something was up but no one was told anything. Not till he called me to his office and broke the news that Erik had been killed. In a landslide.'

'God.' Cassie touched his hand. 'You must have been devastated.'

'Yeah. I mean, he was so young, so intelligent, so full of promise and potential. Beautiful-looking, of course. He was one of the Few, after all. I suppose I had a little bit of a crush on him. Still, he had a lifetime's happiness and success ahead of him.' Patrick stared at the tablecloth. 'And it was all gone, just like that. Surreal.'

The silence that fell wasn't uncomfortable. It felt quite appropriate. At last, Patrick looked up and nodded to the hovering waiter.

'I always wondered what they were looking for, out

there in the Yucatán.' He shrugged. 'But Sir Alric never said. I suppose, after Erik died, it was irrelevant. Now.' He sat up, trying to look more cheerful, and smiled at the waiter. 'Are you ready to order, Cassie?'

When they'd chosen – Cassie with some difficulty, since she wanted at least five of the things on the menu – Patrick shook his head and smiled more positively. 'Let's not talk about sad things any more, eh? I want to hear what you've been up to here this term. Any nice boys? Whatever happened with that Ran—'

'Uh, we're not talking about him,' she interjected, with a slightly stiff smile.

'Ah.' Patrick nodded. 'Fair enough! I'll stick to safer subjects. What's the Academy building like? We never came to this one while I was a student.'

Cassie smiled, relieved he didn't press her any further on romance. 'It's pretty spectacular actually. Certainly a far cry from Cranlake.'

'I don't doubt it! Well, tell me all about it, and while you're at it, give me some gossip about the teachers. Some of them haven't changed since my day, you know.'

'Yeah, the ones with the cobwebs hanging off their eyebrows might be familiar to you,' she ribbed.

'Hey! I'm not that old!'

As Patrick began to list off some of the teachers he'd

had while he was at the Academy, Cassie sighed contentedly. One thing was sorted at least. Giggling at his irreverent comments, Cassie realised with a huge sense of relief how much she'd missed him. Thank God she'd sent that text. This was just what she'd needed, a connection to her old life. She wouldn't forget it, or him, just because of this new start of hers. He was family.

Now all she needed to do was kick Ranjit out of her thoughts for good, and she'd be sorted.

CHAPTER SIX

The long weekend that Patrick had spent in Istanbul seemed to fly by – before Cassie knew it, she'd been seeing him off at the airport. Great as it was to see him, Cassie was oddly pleased to fully re-immerse herself back into Academy life. As she walked through the courtyard, just the trickling splash of water in the fountain made her feel cooler in the summer heat. She paused, books in her arms, smiling up at the statue of Leda and her swan against the open sky. She got fonder and fonder of the poor girl, seduced by that savage beautiful bird. Cassie knew exactly how she felt . . .

Nah, she told herself firmly. Leda should have dumped that swan. Or better still, wrung its scrawny neck.

She'd like to wring Ranjit's, that was for sure. Funny how, for all his grandiose declarations, she'd seen barely hide nor hair of him in the past few days. His new devotion to her obviously wasn't interfering with his old habit of skipping half his classes. Maybe he was off like Indiana Jones, finding the solution to all their problems. Yeah, right.

'Cassie!'

She turned and was surprised by the genuine feeling of happiness she felt when she saw who was coming towards her. Richard's insolent grin was infectious, and she couldn't help but return it as he sauntered across the courtyard. When he reached her, he aimed a kiss at Cassie's cheek and seemed a little surprised when she let it connect.

'You looked like you were struggling a bit in there,' she joked, gesturing back towards Herr Stolz's classroom.

'Bloody hell, you're telling me,' he said, making a show of trying to get air down his collar. 'Maths was purgatory today, Bell, I don't know how you do it.'

She raised an eyebrow. 'Wouldn't have been such a struggle if you'd done the prep, mate.'

'Agreed. Might have stopped Stolz getting his lederhosen in a twist. Anyway, that's enough about the daily grind,' he said, looking up at the gleaming marble figures. 'How about these statues, eh? Don't you think Io would be more appropriate here instead of Leda? I don't know if you know the story, but that naughty Zeus has a lot to answer for here in Istanbul—'

'I *do* know, as it happens,' Cassie interjected, smiling smugly. 'The old bugger Zeus seduced Io, but his missus got wind of it, so he turned the poor girl into a cow to hide her. But Mrs Z wasn't fooled, she sent a bee to sting the heifer in her rear. And Io bolted and paddled as fast as her hooves could carry her across the strait – hence, the Bosphorus, meaning "passage of the cow". Hah!'

Richard pushed his hair out of his eye sheepishly. 'Right, you obviously *do* do your homework! Beautiful, and intelligent too.'

Cassie flushed unexpectedly at the compliment. 'Well, uh, I swatted up cos I wanted to be the one making sinister remarks about pagan deities this year,' she joked, recovering. He chuckled, and Cassie noticed he had dimples. Had she noticed those before? Keep talking, Cassie, she thought. 'Anyway, don't you think there's a bit of a god-obsession round here? I'm sure it's what makes the Few so . . .'

'Up ourselves?' finished Richard.

Cassie grinned; couldn't help it. 'Yeah.'

Thinking about Isabella's shameless matchmaking, she studied him again as he fiddled absent-mindedly with the trailing tendrils of a black orchid on the stone of the pool. There was no point denying it. Richard *was* bloody good-looking, and a charmer, and he had those green eyes and that sexy mouth . . .

But no. It would be crazy to fall for someone so flaky. And sometimes Cassie wasn't sure if his 'anything goes' attitude might not work in her favour. Who knows, she thought, he might be more into guys? What if girls were just a change of scene for him? An occasional holiday? Not that she was thinking of being his weekend break. Not seriously anyway . . . Flaky! she reminded herself. Unreliable, changeable, flippant . . . But then again, there were those cheekbones, as defined as his arm muscles . . . Oh, stop it, Cassie!

Richard glanced up at her through his dark lashes. 'Hey, Cassie?' He hesitated. 'I appreciate it, you know.'

'What?'

'You forgiving me.'

'Well, now I didn't say I'd forgiven you.' She cocked an eyebrow. 'It's just with Isabella still a little down in the dumps, if I don't talk to you then I might end up missing out on some of the school gossip.'

He grinned rakishly. 'Well by all means, let me share some. What are you doing with your free afternoon? Want to come to Beyoglu? I know this—'

'Perfect little café?' she mimicked dryly, recalling his fateful words from her first term at the Academy. 'Uh-huh. No thanks. Besides, I was thinking something cultural. The Blue Mosque, maybe.'

He looked injured. 'Hey, I can do culture, Ms Bell. I could show you the— uh-oh.' At the sound of footsteps clicking on the tiles he'd glanced past her, shooting a nervous look over her shoulder. Returning his attention to her, Richard winked. 'I think it's time for my cocoa. See you later though, Cassie.'

Staring at him quizzically, she glanced over her shoulder.

Sir Alric Darke.

He was still the same: tall, imposing, with a devilish smile and a scarily intelligent, all-knowing glint in his grey-granite eyes. But she wasn't scared, despite the fact that he was heading their way. He nodded, seeming vaguely amused at Richard's disappearing act.

'Good afternoon, Cassie.'

Well, what had she expected? She was going to have to face him sooner or later, and it might as well be now. Not that she was frightened of him, not any more.

'Hello, Sir Alric.'

'Good to see you back.'

Cassie inwardly scoffed – the comment seemed weighted with extra meaning since the Council of Elders' vote last term. Sir Alric continued. 'How are you finding Istanbul?'

Damn, he was obviously intent on stopping to chat. Biting back on a sarcastic retort, she gave him a tight smile. 'It's very beautiful. What I've seen of it.'

'I'm glad. I hope you'll see a great deal more. Make the most of it.'

'Because I might not have been here at all?' It was out before she could hold her tongue.

He studied her for a few seconds, just long enough to make her uncomfortable.

'Exactly.'

She ought to thank him, she thought as she averted her eyes and stared at the statue. Without his intervention, Cassie would have been in seriously hot water, having unleashed the full force of her unusual power on those unsuspecting bitchy Few girls at Carnegie Hall. This was the moment to say: *Thanks for defending me in front of the Council, Sir Alric. Thanks for having faith in me. Thanks for saving me from the Confine.*

She couldn't; just couldn't. The memory of the price she'd paid – she and Ranjit – was just too bitter. They were not compatible, Sir Alric had said. They could not be together; their spirits were too dangerous, too volatile. He wouldn't have saved her if they'd disobeyed him. No, he'd have let her go to the Confine, imprisoned indefinitely. His help had been conditional on their obedience.

Bastard.

Yes, said Estelle viciously. *Yes, indeed.*

Except that he's probably right, Estelle. Losing Ranjit was for the best. We both know that now . . .

An inner smirk from the spirit, and a strategic silence. Estelle said nothing more.

Breaking the awkward silence, Sir Alric said, 'Cassie, come with me a moment.'

She had no choice but to follow him. He led her beyond the courtyard and along secluded paths through the greenery, but he didn't pause until he reached another, smaller paved courtyard through an arch hung with vines. Filtered sunlight glanced off the panes of a greenhouse, full of propagated black orchids in pots, but he led her straight through that too and into an opulent room that was clearly his office for this term. It was much darker in here, and lamps flickered, making the shadows leap. Did he always have to make his office so damned intimidating? Not for the first time she decided Sir Alric was downright manipulative.

She recognised his usual desk, the lamp, the bookshelves, the antique globe. On a high shelf stood a stunningly carved jade urn that glowed in the dim sunlight from the window. She remembered that from last term, too. She nodded, looking around, as Sir Alric's secretary withdrew discreetly to an anteroom.

'That was not the usual entrance to this office, may I say,' he said by way of an opener. 'As a rule I'd like you to use the corridors.'

'As a rule I will, then.' Shrugging, she said, 'Nice. Made yourself at home already, then. Bit different from New York, though, isn't it?'

'Indeed. I like a change of scene.' Sir Alric smiled, ignoring her frosty tone. 'I like changes altogether. There are many in you, Cassie, if I'm not mistaken. You seem happier. Certainly much better than you did last term.'

'Yeah . . .' she began.

'You're adjusting,' Sir Alric asserted. 'To your status, that is. And may I say, it suits you.'

'Thanks,' she muttered.

'So I take it you'll socialise a little more with the others this term?' His voice was light but there was no mistaking his seriousness. 'It's good for the Few to stick together, and it's never healthy for rivalries to develop. Unfriendly ones, at least. Enmities, shall we say?'

'Yes. Let's.'

Again he ignored her sarcasm. 'Your spirit is a powerful one, Cassie; you know that.'

'Like she ever lets me forget . . .'

'And your particular power entails responsibility.'

'Oh great.' This time she managed to laugh. 'Now I'm Spider Girl.'

He smiled with half his thin mouth. 'I'm not the only one who will be monitoring your progress, Cassie. Please try to keep that in mind. You're here because I persuaded the Council you could integrate. More importantly, that you could control yourself. You won't let me down, I'm sure.' He touched the velvety black petal of an orchid on his desk. 'You're like my plants here: dangerously unique. Your interrupted initiation saw to that. I'm extremely careful when I deal with these orchids, Miss Bell, and I intend to take the same care with you and your turbulent spirit. It's what I promised the Elders, as you will recall.'

'I think I may have some recollection, yes.'

He lifted an eyebrow and met her gaze directly. 'And whether my students approve of them or not, I do keep my promises.'

She couldn't miss the warning in his expression. Once again, he had the moral high ground. 'Yeah. OK.'

'Good,' he said, smiling once more as if they'd just had a perfectly normal student–teacher conversation. He nodded and sat down behind his desk, lifting a folder.

It was a dismissal. The secretary reappeared and held open the door to the anteroom. No pretty greenhouse route this time. Nodding to him, Cassie took a deep breath and left. She walked slowly through the richly wood-panelled corridors, gathering her thoughts.

Damn. Darke always knew how to put a damper on a nice day. Finding that her hands were trembling slightly, she clasped them tighter around her books as she made her way back towards the courtyard.

'Hey.' She felt a light hand on her shoulder. 'Did you get in trouble already, Cassie Bell?'

'Huh?'

Ayeesha smiled and jerked her thumb in the vague direction of Sir Alric's office. 'Saw you got summoned.'

Cassie gave her a weak grin. 'Not really. Just got my card marked, so to speak.'

'Don't let him bother you. He can be a sod, we all know that, but it's only because he worries.'

'Oh, he's a regular sweet old grandpa-figure.' Cassie rolled her eyes, but she couldn't help laughing. Ayeesha joined in.

'Listen, we're having drinks in the Few common room on Thursday. Seven o'clock, to celebrate the start of term. Join us?' Ayeesha raised a hopeful eyebrow.

'Oh! I . . . dunno, I—'

'Don't want to associate with us? Cassie! What could we *possibly* have done to offend you?' She pouted jokily. 'Actually, don't answer that! Just come along anyway?' She grinned. 'We'll make it up to you. Cormac makes a hell of a mojito.'

'Oh, I believe that all right.' Cassie bit her lip. 'But I don't know . . .'

'Hey, look,' Ayeesha said gently. 'All those problems you had last term? Not feeding properly, losing control of yourself? None of that would have happened if we'd been there for you. All the Few, we're supposed to look out for each other, and we didn't.'

Cassie wondered inwardly if Sir Alric had briefed the Bajan girl. 'That wasn't your fault—' she began.

'Well, not entirely, Cassie. But still. We need to make up for what we didn't do.' Ayeesha gave her a beatific grin. 'And some of us do actually like you, despite all your efforts.'

That made Cassie laugh out loud. 'OK, you win! But I don't do committees, right? Nobody's going to try and make me run the Christmas raffle.'

'Nah. We expect you to bake cakes, though, and knit stuffed animals.' Ayeesha winked. 'Seriously, though, you don't have to get any more involved than you want to. We want to be your friends, that's all. It doesn't mean we're all joined at the virtual hip, it's cool. And it'll keep Sir Alric off your back.'

Cassie exhaled deeply. 'That can only be good, I guess! OK, I'll be there.'

'Great!'

'And Ayeesha . . . ? Thanks.'

With a last happy smile, Ayeesha slung her bag on to her shoulder and walked off. Cassie watched her go, unwilling to move till she'd gathered her thoughts, soothed by the echoing trickle and splash of the fountain.

Things were back on track for her plans this term, then. Mean girl Katerina was out of the picture – so was Ranjit, for that matter – and Jake wasn't here, which was rough on Isabella, but certainly made life generally calmer without his revenge-seeking . . . The whole damn scenario was a lot less stressful.

So she was going to make a concerted effort to fit in. What was the point in fighting it? What was the point in resisting Estelle, rejecting her Few existence? There was no going back; everyone had told her so. She could fight it till she dropped dead of boredom and exhaustion, or she could make an effort.

That's my girl, Cassandra. Estelle's voice was soft, and for once she didn't resent it.

That's my girl.

CHAPTER SEVEN

Cassie took a deep breath as she surveyed the students' eager faces around her. She loved field trips, especially here. It wasn't that the Academy itself wasn't a stunningly beautiful place to study and work, but to sail across to Istanbul itself, to see its great architectural jewels up close, was a thrill for Cassie. Besides, perhaps she was a little like Sir Alric in that way: she did like a change of scene. It gave her breathing space, thinking space.

The sounds of the city were somehow muted in the grounds of the stunning Hagia Sophia mosque, softened by the splashing of fountains. Standing on the grass with the rest of the class, Cassie gazed up at its imposing dome and minarets, only half listening to Mr Haswell as he pointed out the Iznik tiling and the delicate beauty of the structure. The sun was warm on the back of her neck and for the moment she didn't take notes, just clasped her book in her arms and basked in the atmosphere.

She was completely relaxed, and she wasn't expecting her neck to prickle with that now-familiar instinct. Frowning, she scratched at the back of her neck and turned.

Where had he appeared from again? She was as sure as she could be that Ranjit had not been on the boat with the rest of them. But he must have been, because now there he was, his eyes locking with hers for a brief moment before he turned away. Nice of him to turn up for a class, she thought sarcastically. And he had been watching her for a while – the tingling of her skin meant nothing else. Now, though, he was blending with the rest of the class as they filed inside the building, his attention apparently intently focused on the soaring space within.

The light beneath the great dome had an almost mystical quality, as if the dome was floating in air. Ranjit gazed up at it, seeming awestruck, then glanced at Cassie across the echoing chamber and broke into a mysterious smile. Cassie only just managed to stop herself smiling in return, because he looked . . . good. Very good. Not as well groomed and polished as usual – in fact he had a downright sloppy look about him, and his jaw was shadowed with stubble – but that only made him more gorgeous. She took a breath, forcing herself to walk away and ignore him.

He didn't try to follow her, and she was glad. As the class broke up into smaller groups, tasked with assignments she hadn't even heard properly, she saw Ranjit break away from the crowd and head off on his own. As he left, he pulled a piece of paper out of his pocket, unfolding it and studying it closely as he walked.

Oh, she was furious with herself. Even as she slipped out of the main building in his wake, she was livid. What was it about her that she couldn't leave the boy alone? Hell, she was curious about what he was up to, that was all. Curious? Fascinated. He had no business sneaking off like that, acting all mysterious and—

He'd come to a halt, beside the remains of an ancient basilica. Cassie stopped too, sidling into the shade of a wall, and she frowned as she watched him. Ranjit was studying the carved stone decorations as if he'd spotted the Holy Grail or something. He glanced around, checking that no one was near; then abruptly, he whisked his phone out of his pocket and started rapidly taking pictures.

Bizarre. She backed away from him, suddenly not wanting him to catch sight of her. Whatever he was up to, she didn't want to know. And she was very reluctant for him to know she'd been watching.

He was striding on now, looking as though butter wouldn't melt in his mouth, making a show of comparing the wall of the former mosque with the photos in his guidebook. Cassie shook her head and turned away. Ranjit and his games were of no interest. At least, they shouldn't be. She should go and find Isabella. What she shouldn't do – no, no, no – was walk across now and investigate what he'd been photographing . . .

Ah, she couldn't help it. Nothing to do with Ranjit, she insisted in her head; it was a natural inquisitiveness. And, you know, maybe he'd seen something interesting and historical. Maybe it was something she ought to see. Or something that might shed some light on what he'd been going on about the other day. Or maybe something worth putting in her project?

Oh, Cassie, stop kidding yourself.

As it turned out, it was a pointless detour. Maybe he just had a stone carving fetish, because there was nothing else of interest on the basilica: elaborate, beautiful patterns etched in the stone, but rubbed to blurry shapes by aeons, and if they'd ever meant anything it was long forgotten. Cassie frowned and shook her head, irritated. She should have known, especially given the nonsense he'd been spouting lately, that it wasn't worth trying to make sense of what Ranjit got up to. Now it really was time to find Isabella.

It wasn't difficult. When she found the front of the huge building again, her friend was just outside the great door, chatting to Mr Haswell.

'Hey, Isabella, there you are. Are we going to check out the script on the walls? Do we have the translations . . . ?' Cassie tailed off as she noticed another tall, too-familiar figure a few metres away. As their eyes met, Sir Alric seemed almost as surprised as she was to see him there. Taking a deep breath, Cassie's heart sank as he walked up to them. She forced a smile.

'Sir Alric. Hi.'

He returned her smile, but his wasn't so over-bright; indeed there was something a little nervous about it.

'Cassie. Mr Haswell.' He nodded a 'hello' to Isabella as well, still looking a little uncomfortable. 'I hadn't realised your history class was coming here today.'

'Yes, it was a late decision,' Mr Haswell said, looking a little worried that perhaps he'd missed some protocol. Cassie couldn't help but grin at him though, suddenly liking him more for putting Sir Alric off his guard. She spoke up.

'How about you, Sir Alric? Doing some research?'

'No. No, I was just taking in the sights myself. I haven't

been in Istanbul for some time.' He gave them all a thin smile. 'You must make the most of your visit, girls. Have you seen all the mosaics?'

'Only the Imperial Gate mosaic so far . . .' began Isabella.

'There are many more. Why don't you seek out the Emperor Alexander mosaic? It's hard to locate, but well worth seeing. On the second floor.' He eyed Cassie and Isabella expectantly, and they glanced at each other. They were dismissed, again.

'And don't forget the *mihrab* in the apse,' called Mr Haswell after them as they headed into the building once more. 'I want a study of the religious past of the museum.'

'Did you ever feel like a primary school kid?' murmured Cassie as they headed off obediently.

Isabella giggled. 'Sir Alric didn't look too happy to find a class here. Probably wanted a peaceful afternoon!'

Yeah, thought Cassie, glancing over her shoulder to see that Sir Alric had taken his leave of Mr Haswell and was striding towards the mausoleums. *Maybe* that's all he wanted. A bit of peace? Somehow she didn't think so, but Cassie didn't care. Whatever was going on with Sir Alric, and Ranjit too, she wasn't getting involved. Not any more.

As far as she could in the Darke Academy, she was going to get through this term as a normal student.

Don't put yourself down, my dear. We're anything but normal.

Cassie smiled wryly. Estelle was right. But she was definitely done with secrets and lies, and wasn't going to let curiosity get the better of her. She'd leave that to some other kitty . . .

CHAPTER EIGHT

'Thank God that's over.' Isabella flung herself backwards on to her bed. 'I have never known such a terrible first week. How many maths classes can a girl stand? And as for chemistry! Chelnikov, he *hates* me!'

'No, he doesn't.' Cassie dumped a pile of books on her desk. 'He kind of likes his lab equipment intact, but he doesn't *hate* you . . .'

'It was an accident!' insisted Isabella, tossing her hair out of her face and sitting up straight. 'Ugh, let us forget the whole catastrophe. Alice suggested we go and try out 360 Istanbul? We can get all the Yusuf gossip from the other side, yes?'

'You're on!' Cassie said, grinning. At least Isabella was proposing doing something fun. But then Cassie's face fell. She'd forgotten . . .

'Damn it. I'm really sorry, I can't. Sorry, Isabella. I

already promised Ayeesha.'

'Promised Ayeesha what?' Isabella frowned.

Cassie felt her cheekbones burn. 'That I'd go to the common room tonight. They're having drinks. Some kind of Few celebration of the start of term.' Her voice trailed off.

Isabella paused for a moment, unable to hide her disappointment.

'Oh, right.'

'Come on, Isabella. It's just a couple of drinks. It's not like they're going to swallow me up.' Cassie bit her lip. 'Listen, maybe I could come and meet you guys afterwards. Or . . . I suppose there's no reason I can't cancel?'

Isabella smiled, though it seemed a little forced. 'No, Cassie, no. This is important for you. You have to socialise, get to know them as well. Really, don't worry. It's OK.'

Cassie felt even worse, now that Isabella was being so sweet about it. 'I don't know . . .'

'You're to go to your drinks. Really. I'll tell you all about the restaurant later.' She gave Cassie a sly grin. 'It's very beautiful, though, apparently. Views right across the city and the sea, I hear . . .'

'Don't,' groaned Cassie. 'I'd rather be coming with you guys, honest.'

'Next time, then.' Isabella jumped up and began rummaging through her wardrobe. 'Now let me see. For such a special place I should dress up. Maybe the Hussein Chalayan . . . ?'

'Stop it!' Cassie flopped on to her bed, wishing heartily that she'd never accepted Ayeesha's invitation, that she was going out on the town with her best friend and Alice instead. Then she jumped as she felt her phone vibrate.

Cassie tugged it out of her jeans pocket and peered at the caller ID. Shocked, she snatched a quick glance at Isabella. The girl was still in a trance of indecision, holding a dress against herself and frowning into the mirror.

Ranjit Singh, said the display.

'Now what the hell do you want?' Cassie murmured at the phone. She took a deep shaky breath, and then deliberately slid the phone back into her pocket. No way. Not when she was already feeling so bad about letting Isabella down. Not when she was so nervous about her visit to the common room, which was, oh *yes*, just the sort of occasion on which Ranjit would have found a way to let her down.

She left the phone to continue vibrating, and gave a sigh of relief when it finally stopped.

* * *

She lasted remarkably well, Cassie told herself later. Showed amazing restraint, all things considered. It was a whole hour before she finally gave in and responded to that insistent bleep of the voicemail message. Even then it was only after Estelle's insistence that she should prepare herself in case Ranjit had something planned when she got to the drinks.

Closing the door of their room, pausing in the corridor, she shut her eyes and sighed. Of course she had to listen. Get it over with. She wouldn't ever relax for her imminent common room ordeal otherwise . . .

Flipping the phone open before she could change her mind, she punched in the number and pressed the phone to her ear.

'Cassie.' Ranjit's voice sounded breathless on the voicemail, desperate. 'Cassie, I know why you won't answer, but hear me out. Please.' A shaky breath. But there was more than nerves in his voice, she thought, frowning. There was high, repressed excitement.

'Meet me at seven, OK? My room. No pressure, I promise. I know— Listen, I know you don't trust me any more. Fair enough. I let you down, but I want to make up for that, I really do.' A bark of awkward laughter. 'God, it's just so lucky we're in Istanbul this year! Believe me, Cassie, I can fix this. I WILL fix this. I'm nearly there. Soon I'll be able to . . . to heal *old wounds, if you like.'* A pause, then another high ironic laugh. *'Or maybe I should say "break old ties"!'*

He hesitated again, as if he wanted to say more, and she pressed the phone closer to her ear, so close that it hurt. But there was nothing else. After a few seconds, the line went dead.

Heal old wounds? What was that supposed to mean? Apart from being melodramatic guff to get her to his room, she thought angrily. Break old ties? Arsehole!

Then she thought about Estelle, about the broken state of her spirit, the part of it that remained outside Cassie, and shuddered . . .

She didn't know which was more powerful, the rage at his cheek, or the unbearable curiosity. Well, no, that wasn't true. Of course the curiosity was going to win out. He knew that, didn't he? Which, she thought as she stormed to his room in the upper corridor, made her even more furious.

I'm not sure this is such a good idea, Cassandra . . .

Cassie ignored Estelle's cautious interjection. As she hesitated in front of his door, she checked her watch. Two minutes past seven. Not nearly long enough to keep him waiting, but it would have to do. She had things to do, places to be. She wasn't hanging about for Ranjit.

Her knock must have sounded as if she was trying to break down the door.

It flew open. Not Ranjit, she realised, taking a surprised step back. Torvald, his roommate. She wasn't expecting that.

Clearly, neither was Torvald. He looked a little bemused.

'Cassie? Hey. What's up?'

'Hey. Is Ranjit in there? I got a message from him.'

'No . . .' said Torvald. 'Actually, I don't know where he is. But, you know, it's not like I've got him electronically tagged,' he added smiling dryly. 'Maybe you were mistaken?'

Cassie was confused. 'But he asked me to meet him here.'

Torvald's brow furrowed. 'Listen, Cassie. It's not really any of my business, but you're not still leading him on, are you?'

Cassie blinked hard, shocked and angered by the irony of the statement. She took a breath. 'What?'

'Well, it's just that he hasn't been the same since you guys broke up. He's even more serious.' Rolling his eyes, he added, 'If that's possible . . .'

She bristled. 'He asked *me* to meet *him*.'

'Yeah? Well, he's not here. Honestly, I've no idea

where he's gone.' He shrugged.

Cassie hesitated, then shook her head. 'I just don't get him,' she muttered.

'If it's any help, he's been *really* screwed up since you dumped him. I don't really get him either, lately.'

He dumped *me*! she wanted to yell, but there wasn't any point. It wasn't Torvald's fault. 'Well, just tell him I didn't wait about, right?'

'OK, sure.'

Walking away, she turned on her heel and swallowed her anger for a second. 'Tell him . . . I'll be in the common room if he wants to talk.'

CHAPTER NINE

Livid as Cassie was at Ranjit's stupid mind games, at least the irritation distracted from her nerves as she approached the common room. Outside it, lights glowed in wrought-iron sconces, and the solid door looked very forbidding. Cassie lifted her fist and hammered on the dark, carved wood.

Might have been a little violent, she thought, swallowing hard as the door swung open to reveal the faces of the Few, turned towards her with expressions that ranged from curiosity to mild surprise to outright hostility. Avoiding their stares, she noticed the room was opulent, rich with coloured glass, gilded archways and expensive *kilims*, and the light was soft and glowing. Windows stood open to the gardens beyond; she could smell the salty breeze mixed with the dusky scent of geraniums.

'Cassie!'

Thank God for a friendly face. Ayeesha hurried up and embraced her warmly.

'I'm so glad you came. *We're* so glad!' Ayeesha's glance at several of her comrades held a touch of defiance. 'Come in, have a drink. You know everyone by now, I think. Or, no – come and meet Saski. She's a third year, I don't know if you met her yet . . .'

Cassie gave Saski a sympathetic smile, but the girl didn't seem anything but triumphantly excited about her new status. Cassie diffused her vision as they chatted, focusing on the spirit nestling within the girl's chest. A mildly powerful aura with an element of wickedness, or perhaps just mischief. Cassie let her attention fall on each Few member in turn as she relaxed and chatted. They were as she remembered them. The strong and the weak; the bad and the genuinely good. The spirits were as usual clustered according to their characters, and the more timid ones were gravitating to the protection of the more powerful. One of the strongest of them all, however, was still nowhere to be seen. That made her even more curious. Ranjit could be stand-offish, but even if he hadn't kept his own appointment with her, Cassie did half expect him to impose his presence on the start-of-term party: mark his territory, so to speak.

'Has Ranjit been by?' she asked Ayeesha casually.

'No.' Ayeesha blinked, as though she'd only just realised. 'No, he hasn't. I assume he's coming along later, though?'

Cassie shrugged. 'I dunno.'

'Oh! Oh, I see. So, you're not . . . . I wasn't sure if—'

'No. We're not.'

Ayeesha's face fell. 'I'm sorry about that, Cassie. I really am. You and he were—'

'Yes,' interrupted Cassie. 'But it's over. Totally over.' And she wasn't going to spend another second fretting about Ranjit's tomfoolery.

Ayeesha hesitated, and then smiled apologetically. 'OK. Sorry, of course. Look, why don't you come over and talk to Yusuf and India? They're always good value.'

Cassie wasn't sure she agreed. The two older Few students seemed a little distant – Yusuf clearly thought the world of himself, and he had a predatory soulmate in India. They were too busy discussing their latest romantic conquests to include Cassie much in their conversation, but they were pretty funny at the same time, and at least they weren't openly hostile like Mikhail and Sara. She could feel *those* glares burning a hole between her shoulder blades, though from the English girl it was understandable, given the lashing Cassie had given her last term, when the unusual 'ability' she possessed first reared its invisible head.

Still, Cassie wasn't thinking about the past, and she definitely wasn't planning to give any more thought to the likes of Sara, or indeed Ranjit bloody Singh. No. She was having fun. She was enjoying being single. And ready to tingle, as Isabella might say.

So heaven only knew why she couldn't keep her eyes off the carved door. Heaven knew why she kept aching for it to open, for a familiar beautiful figure to appear, and smile, and walk up to her, and *apologise*, damn it! What was he playing at, anyway? She'd never been stood up for a meeting she hadn't even requested before, and it really wasn't flattering.

Speaking of which . . .

When the door finally did swing open, it wasn't the figure she was expecting, but it was a welcome one nonetheless. Richard. If anyone at this soirée was going to make her feel better, it was probably going to be him, she thought, with only a hint of grudging. As he headed towards her, elegantly swerving past other Few members, a glass miraculously in each hand, she was ambushed by a huge sense of gratitude.

'Hey, Cassie,' he said, eyeing her with an appreciative grin. 'Enjoying the party? Would you like me to get the knives out of your back so you can sit down?'

Laughing, she took the drink he proffered. 'Cheers, mate. I think can manage them.'

'I don't doubt it, Ms Bell.' Richard glanced over her shoulder. 'Sara and her posse are livid. It's fantastic.' He leaned a little closer. 'Of course, we could get them talking some more . . .'

'You have so got to stop that. You could lead a girl on, you know.' She attempted a sarcastic smile, but found herself taking a step back, still a little alarmed by the attraction she was feeling towards him. And the way his shirt skimmed over the muscles in his chest . . .

'Really?' Richard asked innocently – or was it hopefully? Cassie flushed a little.

'Well, to be honest, I didn't think I was really your type. I was under the impression that maybe you were, uh, playing more for the other team . . . ?'

He laughed. 'Ah. I've got a theory on that actually: before my induction into our esteemed little gang here, I was strictly het. I reckon it's just my pesky spirit who likes to play away – I assure you that I'm most certainly on your team. Or I'd like to be,' he added, raising his eyebrows.

Cassie gaped at him for a moment, and then couldn't help bursting out laughing as well. 'You're joking.'

'I'm not.'

'Isn't that a bit . . . *inconvenient*?'

'Oh, I don't know. I've always thought of myself as a bit of a try-sexual anyway, so hey, why not? Best of both worlds, that's how I look at it.' A mischievous smile spread across his lips.

'Lordy, I did wonder.' Cassie laughed again, shaking her head. 'You're a boy of two halves.'

'And both of them highly attractive. Now come on, Cassie. Let's party.'

It had been fine. More than fine, in fact. She'd had great fun in the end – who could avoid it with Richard around? Besides, if Ranjit *had* turned up, what would she have said to him?

Still, back at her room, she'd had a restless night with little sleep, and it was mostly because of him. Who stood up an ex-girlfriend – one he was supposedly pining for, according to his roommate – when *he* was the one who'd suggested they meet? It was for the best really anyway. They'd only have quarrelled. Yes, they'd have had one of their ear-splitting, animal-scaring rows, and if he'd turned up at the common room then it would have been right in front of the rest of the Few. She couldn't have stood that.

Still . . .

It would have been reassuring just to catch sight of him, but Ranjit stayed resolutely absent from all his classes the next day. There was no sign of him, but Cassie refused to worry. It wasn't as if he hadn't cut lessons before; he made an absolute habit of it. The boy was a law unto himself.

Still . . .

The last lesson of the day, and the heat in the classroom was suffocating despite the gently turning fans overhead. Madame Lefevre's sonorous but soporific voice wasn't helping, and Cassie just couldn't concentrate. A dove had settled on the windowsill by the latticed shutters, and at least its cooing was soothing. She tried to focus on the bird instead, but her eyes kept drifting beyond it to the leafy gardens. Was he out there?

She was relieved when the interminable day was over, and glad too for the cool of the evening. Returning to her room and throwing her bag down on to her bed, she almost jumped when Isabella stuck her head round the bathroom door and cheerfully called out.

'Cassie! Hey! How was your afternoon?'

Cassie did a double take, and then smiled. 'Hi! You're in a good mood.' An unusually good mood for Isabella, these days . . .

Isabella looked almost shifty for a moment, but then

she grinned. Ducking back into the bathroom, she reappeared clutching a bottle that looked sculpted out of crystal. The amber liquid within had an almost nuclear glow. 'New shampoo. So expensive, and who knows what it does for my hair, but it makes *me* very, very happy.'

'Just the price tag makes you happy?' Cassie tilted an eyebrow, nevertheless ridiculously pleased as her friend beamed back.

'You know nothing makes me happier than spending my inheritance on supporting the economy, Cassie.' Isabella winked. 'Listen, how do you fancy hanging out this weekend? We haven't really spent any time together properly this term. It could be like old times, no? Just like old times . . .' She muttered the last sentence to herself, but seemed to stop when she caught Cassie's quizzical look. What had brought all this on?

'How about it?' Isabella continued.

'Isabella, that sounds wonderful.' Cassie felt a surge of relief, despite the sudden nature of Isabella's new-found good mood. She hadn't seen her friend this happy since . . . Well, since last term.

'It does, doesn't it?' Isabella agreed, nodding happily.

Cassie returned her friend's enthusiastic grin, though she couldn't shake the feeling it was all a bit odd. First Ranjit, now Isabella acting bizarrely. Well, all in a day's work at the Academy, she thought, chuckling to herself. Anyway, so what? All that mattered was that Isabella was cheerful again, almost back to her normal self, and Cassie wasn't going to question that too hard.

So long as Isabella was finding her way back, she didn't care. Cassie had missed her far, far too much to rock the boat now . . .

CHAPTER TEN

As Isabella dumped her bag on her desk and sat down, Cassie glanced around the history class. There seemed to be more of a buzz than usual, more furtive whispered comments and suppressed excitement. Even among the Few, in their usual spot at the back of the room, there was a flicker of nervous energy.

Mr Haswell was calling for quiet, asking them to take their seats, but Cassie was Few, wasn't she? She didn't often pull rank, and never usually around the teachers, but now was perhaps the time to start. She headed straight for the back of the class and leaned down to talk to Ayeesha.

'He just never came back,' Ayeesha's neighbour Lara was saying. 'Nobody knows what's happened.'

Cassie interrupted. 'There's no need to panic though, is there? I mean, Ranjit's been away before.'

Lara blinked and shook her head. 'What are you talking about?'

'It's no big deal,' muttered Cassie. 'Why's everyone making a big thing of it?'

'It isn't Ranjit,' explained Ayeesha. 'We all know what *he's* like; skips class all the time. It's Yusuf.'

For a moment Cassie felt like she'd fallen into a parallel world. 'What?'

'Yusuf Ahmed,' said Lara patiently, as if there was another Yusuf in school. 'He didn't come back to the Academy last night. No sign of him this morning. People are beginning to wonder.'

Cassie laughed. 'You're worried about *Yusuf*? He probably fell asleep in some poor damsel's bed, and right now he's being thrashed by her irate father!'

Ayeesha didn't laugh. 'I don't think so. They found his wallet near the docks at Sultanahmet. His credit cards, his cash: everything gone.'

Cassie didn't know what else to say, and Mr Haswell was getting downright impatient now. She walked back to the front of the class and took her seat next to Isabella.

Yusuf had lost his wallet. So what? He could have dropped it. Unlikely, but even more unlikely that he'd come to grief from a mugger. He was Few, for heaven's sake! It would be the thief who was sorry.

So he'd lost it somewhere else. A thief had found it, emptied it, dumped it. That was the only explanation.

It's not our concern, my dear!

She's right, Cassie thought. It wasn't really anything to do with her. And it was probably nothing anyway. Yusuf could take care of himself.

Yet, she couldn't help thinking . . . There'd been no sign of Ranjit for the past couple of days, and now Yusuf had disappeared too? That was a bit of an odd coincidence. Could their absences be connected? The thought lodged in her brain like a lead weight, despite her efforts to shake it free.

Torvald: had he maybe heard something? If she could speak to him, then perhaps she could settle the matter once and for all – especially as she'd promised herself no more worrying about Ranjit. And she wasn't worried, was she? She just wanted to clear things up.

After class she ran to catch up with Torvald, but Mr Haswell caught her with a query about a homework assignment. By the time Cassie eased herself free, she'd missed Torvald by a whisker, and she had no idea what his next subject was.

Oh, forget it. What could she do anyway? And in any case, she didn't want Torvald to tell Ranjit she was desperately looking for him, or worried about him. There was a good chance that Ranjit was *trying* to make her anxious, playing some warped manipulative game. She wouldn't put it past him, and she certainly wouldn't indulge him.

Quite right, my dear. Ignore him!

Gospodin Chelnikov was less inclined to indulge the mutter of gossip than Mr Haswell had been. As the students filed into the chemistry lab, the Russian clapped his hands, his blue eyes so cold and fierce that even the Few sat down with little fuss.

'Quiet, all of you. I know there are some rumours circulating concerning Yusuf Ahmed. It's natural for you all to be concerned, but Sir Alric has asked me to speak to you about this, as it is beginning to disrupt today's classes.'

'How do you explain—' interrupted someone at the front.

'He hasn't yet been missing for twenty-four hours,' snapped Chelnikov. 'The school has notified the authorities that a student did not return to the school last night. That is the only action that needs to be taken now. Yusuf has an adventurous nature, so it may well be that his night simply caught up with him.'

A few titters ran round the classroom, and Chelnikov very nearly cracked a smile.

'But what about his wallet, sir?'

'Perhaps he lost it in circumstances he's embarrassed to admit. Now, all speculation will *cease*, at least in my classroom. Do you understand?'

He was right, thought Cassie as she tried to focus on her textbook. Yusuf was adventurous. Ranjit, meanwhile, she was sure now, was simply trying to worry or hurt her. She'd given Ranjit a pretty harsh kiss-off the other night; maybe he thought that if he scared her enough, she'd come around. That she'd magically realise she missed him, and agree to go along with his plan . . . Oh, who knew? Cassie really didn't know what to think.

Isabella, however, wasn't so uncertain when they left the class together. 'This is crazy,' she said firmly. 'Two students vanishing into thin air? Something's not right. The school should do something.'

'What would they do? Look, you heard Gospodin Chelnikov. Yusuf hasn't even been missing that long. And he's a risky type. He'll be back. Ranjit too.'

'I'm a little surprised you are so complacent,' sniffed Isabella. 'Especially with Ranjit one of those missing. I mean, aren't you worried at all? If it was me . . .'

Cassie sighed in exasperation. 'Look, Ranjit isn't even my boyfriend any more. It's not up to me to chase him around! Of course I'm worried but there's not much I can do about it, is there? I'm sure he'll turn up and then I'll just be left feeling foolish.'

'All right, Cassie, all right. Let's not fight about it.' Isabella linked her arm through Cassie's. 'Why don't we go somewhere on the mainland? Do something to take our minds off it all?'

'Well, funny you should mention, actually. Uh, Ayeesha and some of the others were talking about going across to Beyoglu.' Cassie cleared her throat, embarrassed again. 'You know, hang around Cukurcuma, do some shopping. Shall we go with them? I kind of said I'd go . . .'

'Oh, how could I *possibly* resist hanging out with the Few? I could carry their shopping bags.'

Cassie raised an eyebrow at her roommate's snarky tone. 'You sound just like—'

'Hmm?'

. . . *Jake*, thought Cassie, finishing her sentence in her head. Even with Isabella's improved outlook, it probably wouldn't be tactful to mention him, especially if she was trying to persuade her friend to come along with them to the mainland. Instead, Cassie grinned.

'Anyway, don't be stupid. We'll probably have to club together to carry yours! But listen, seriously, Isabella, I won't go if you don't fancy it.'

'In *that* case . . .' Isabella paused, then laughed. 'No, come on, let's go!'

This hadn't exactly gone to plan, Cassie had to admit to herself as the six of them negotiated the busy, chic little streets of Cukurcuma. Things had started off OK as they explored the sleek, modern, glass-fronted furniture warehouses which butted up against the historical buildings of sand-coloured stone, and she'd been enjoying looking at the beautiful, vivid upholstery materials piled high in antique stores together with vintage marble basins and intricately weaved carpets. But it was becoming increasingly apparent that Isabella was starting to feel a bit left out in the midst of Cassie's attempts to integrate more with the Few.

'What about this vanity table, ladies?' India said as she eyed a beautifully carved dresser in a small boutique off one of the cobbled streets.

'Seems appropriate,' Isabella said, barely making an effort to keep her comment under her breath. Cassie gave her a warning glance.

'Yeah, looks good,' she said, ignoring her friend.

India gritted her teeth, visibly annoyed by Isabella's snipe, and turned to the other Few girls. 'I'll get it shipped back home then, shall I?' She wandered off towards the store owner, credit card in hand.

Cassie cringed. Some of Isabella's mild snarkiness was starting at times to turn into outright confrontation, and she felt a little caught in the middle. The other girls weren't exactly being as inclusive as they could have been, to be fair. All in all, the tension was putting a strain on the outing. Cassie had begun to regret inviting Isabella a little. But just thinking that gave her a jolt of guilt. After all Isabella had done for her. After all Isabella had sacrificed . . .

Mind you, at least Isabella wasn't looking so miserable now. There was a sharpness and a spark to her moodiness that was oddly reassuring – more like the old, feisty Isabella – even if it was a little unnerving. Her attitude reminded Cassie more and more of how confident and spirited Isabella had been in previous, happier terms, when a certain someone was the focus of almost all her energies. In fact, if she didn't know any better, Cassie would think Jake had been in touch with her roommate . . .

But of course he hadn't. Cassie would have known soon enough if he had. Isabella would have woken her up at two am, jumping for joy on her head.

Still, an atmosphere was an atmosphere, and she could have cut the one between her and her roommate with a blunt knife. But she had to befriend the Few, and Isabella knew that. Besides, some of them were really decent people, like Ayeesha. Cassie respected them, she liked them, and it wasn't really as if she had a choice in any case. Isabella could surely understand that?

Cassie couldn't even use retail therapy as a means of distraction in the way that the other rich girls at the Academy could. While they gasped and giggled over yet another mind-blowing, wallet-defying handbag, and Isabella made critical comments about their taste, Cassie tried to focus only on her surroundings. Something besides the tense atmosphere between the girls was making her uneasy, but she couldn't quite put her finger on what it was. A certain movement, something pricking her senses, but she couldn't think what.

Estelle, she thought, can you feel that?

Yes, my dear, came the anxious reply, but Cassie's 'conversation' was interrupted by more bickering amongst the girls. She convinced herself that it couldn't be anything too serious, or Estelle would have alerted her to it sooner. Anyway, it was silly, because this part of town was outrageously pretty. The lanes wound down steps between old houses with prettily painted shutters and window boxes that overflowed with geraniums. Yet all Cassie could think was that the splashes of scarlet looked so much like spattered blood. When a petal drifted down to the cobbled street, she found herself dodging it.

And then she felt it.

A watcher.

She turned, narrowing her eyes.

No way. She was imagining things; her nerves were shot, that was all. She was on edge because of Isabella and – oh, everything else. Who'd be trailing her round Cukurcuma? It couldn't be . . . ? With a mixture of hope and irritation, she waited to feel that familiar prickling sensation, but she wasn't sure. Was it there? Was she just on edge and imagining it? Estelle remained unhelpfully silent. Perhaps it wasn't Ranjit then, she thought, irritated at her disappointment.

But then who?

Cassie forced herself to take an interest in the discussion about Umit Unal's latest gowns, aware she was being hyper-cheerful, and ridiculously keen to draw Isabella and the Few girls into a simultaneous, friendly conversation. And trying to forget that feeling too – that between-the-shoulder-blades, indefinable itch. Falling silent for a moment and drawing away from the gaggle of girls, Cassie turned slightly to peer over her shoulder. Again, nobody was there.

But no. She was sure she'd been right the first time.

The force of the stare was almost tangible. There was no way, with her heightened Few senses, she could be mistaken. She could even tell where it was coming from. Behind and to the right.

She raised her head to search the shuttered windows, but the sun was in her eyes and he was downwind, whoever he was. Her entire body went still.

Somebody's watching us . . .

We're imagining things, Cassie insisted unconvincingly to herself and to Estelle, shaking her head fiercely. She couldn't see anyone.

And hard on the heels of that thought, she wondered why she kept trying to talk herself out of her own instincts.

CHAPTER ELEVEN

Guilt, my old friend, Cassie thought. There you are again. It was partly Isabella's sulkiness, she told herself. If the girl hadn't started getting so moody about her doing what she *had* to do, Cassie might not even have hung out so much with the Few. As it was, she found she was enjoying their company more and more over the past few days, despite it making her feel doubly bad about Isabella.

Gathering her strength as the students sprang up when the lunch bell sounded, Cassie decided to make an effort to hang out with her roommate after their art class.

'Isabella,' Cassie said, turning to her friend. 'Wanna grab some lunch?'

Isabella gave a quick, distracted smile. 'Yeah, just a sec.' She turned as Alice tapped her on the shoulder, and they began a quick chat.

'Cassie!' Cormac called. 'Coming to the common room?'

'Actually,' Ayeesha interjected, 'I think we should head to the cafeteria today. The chef from that great restaurant, Rami, is guesting today, and his hünkar begendi is my favourite!'

'Oh, definitely!' Cormac said, smacking his lips as he took his girlfriend's hand.

'Cassie?' Ayeesha said expectantly.

'Uh, hang on. I should wait for Isabella.' Cassie looked back towards the classroom, where Isabella was still chatting to Alice.

'Oh, yeah. Fair enough.'

Cassie watched as the pair joined with some more Few students and made their way down the corridor. She sighed. Most days now after classes – with which she was making a much bigger effort, since it (nearly) stopped her thinking about anything else – Cassie found herself hanging out with the Few, and she almost felt regretful that she'd said she'd wait behind. The common room, for example, had begun to feel more and more like a haven: enclosed, secret, safe. The little luxuries it offered didn't do any harm either. Of course, there were still people there who loathed her, but it was surprising how easy it was to ignore them. They didn't even bother her any more; she found she could ignore their glares and exist in a bubble of superiority that drove them half demented. She knew she and, most importantly, her spirit were the equal of any of them, and better than most. She didn't have to care. And of course, there were plenty of them she liked.

When Isabella finally wrapped up her conversation with Alice and returned her attention to Cassie, there was a slightly awkward silence as they made their way over to the cafeteria. Cassie frowned at the thought that she wouldn't be able to speak easily with her friend. She cleared her throat.

'So, what was Alice saying?'

'Oh, more boy trouble,' Isabella said, smiling a kind of private smile that made Cassie feel oddly excluded.

'Right. As usual.' She couldn't resist a dismissive tone. It seemed as though Isabella was more interested in what Alice got up to at the moment than what was going on with her supposed best friend. Luckily, Cassie's rather stormy mood brightened when they reached the cafeteria and she saw the table of Few gesticulating for her to join them.

'Look, there are the guys,' she said with a wave, and began to make her way over automatically.

'Um . . .' Isabella began, hesitating.

'What's up?'

Isabella glanced over to another table, where Alice and another girl were sitting. 'It's just . . . well if you were going to sit with Ayeesha and everyone again, then maybe I might go and make sure Alice is OK?'

'Oh. Right. Yeah if you'd prefer . . .' Cassie said, trying not to look hurt. What was it with Isabella lately? She was trying her best to include her, but she just wouldn't bite.

'Well, yeah. But I'll see you later though, right?'

'Yeah, see you later.' Cassie tried to force a smile and what she hoped passed for a jovial wave, ignoring the strange sensation of she and Isabella walking to opposite sides of the room to be with other friends. Well, they weren't joined at the hip, were they?

'Hey, guys,' Cassie said as she made her way over to the Few table, but she couldn't inject much enthusiasm into her voice.

'Cassie! Grab a tray. Seriously, this chef is amazing,' Ayeesha enthused.

'Yeah, I'm not really hungry,' she replied, irritation bubbling up inside her.

Ah, but we will be, my dear. You know I'm all for asserting our position amongst the others, but we must be careful to keep our feeding source happy . . .

Cassie frowned at Estelle's interjection. She was

annoyed enough at how the day was going without her putting her two pennies' worth in. All she'd done was jump through hoops to keep everyone happy, *especially* Isabella. But she had to draw the line somewhere, concentrate on her own happiness. If that meant hanging around with the Few, then Isabella would just have to lump it.

OK, there was the Jake and Jessica thing. OK, so Isabella still felt loyal to Jake and his crazy quest for justice – or his definition of it. But it wasn't as if the likes of Ayeesha or India had had anything to do with his sister Jessica's murder. Of the girls who had actually done it, one was dead, and one expelled and scarred for life. Katerina and Keiko didn't represent the whole of the Few, for goodness' sake. The Few were so much more than a couple of twisted individuals like them.

Cassie was just shaking herself from her internal rant when a shadow fell over their small group at the table.

'Ladies.'

'Sir Alric.' India raised her eyebrows in surprise. 'It's unusual to see you here.' She smiled tentatively, glancing at the boys animatedly play fighting at the other end of the table.

He nodded. 'I thought I might take a sample of the food as we have a guest in the kitchen today.'

'Yes, indeed. Delicious.' Ayeesha couldn't get the puzzled look off her face, and Cassie couldn't agree more. She didn't like the way Sir Alric kept glancing over at her, inquisition burning behind his eyes.

'How are classes going?'

Funny question in the middle of lunchtime, thought Cassie, though India and Ayeesha seemed eager to take this rare opportunity to impress their elusive headmaster. If only her own conversations with Sir Alric were so infrequent. She eyed him closely as the girls around her chattered their responses enthusiastically. He narrowed his eyes once more at her, though he ostensibly addressed all three of them.

'I see Mr Singh is still not gracing us with his presence.'

'Maybe one of the boys might know where he is? Better than we do, anyway,' India said, glancing down to Cormac and his friends.

'I doubt that. In any case, boys are not as sensitive to things as you are, am I right? I thought some of you ladies might have an instinct about where he's been lately.'

Cassie couldn't help noticing he was once again looking almost exclusively at her. She felt a creeping uneasiness – was he accusing her of something?

'You know as well as I— as well as we all do. Ranjit's a law unto himself. It's hardly unusual that he's cutting classes, always has. That's not our fault. He comes and goes as he pleases. Stands people up when he feels like it, too,' she added bitterly.

Even some of the Few girls looked shocked at the way she spoke to Sir Alric, but he wasn't baited.

'Well, I'll keep an eye out,' he said lightly. 'No doubt our elusive friend will turn up sooner or later.' His intense gaze bored into Cassie. 'But if you do happen to spot him, tell him I would like a brief word.'

As soon as Sir Alric had gone, Cassie made her excuses, said goodbye to the other girls and headed for her room. He'd managed to rile her, and worse, he'd reawakened all her anxieties. On top of everything else, she was growing more and more alarmed about the state of her relationship with Isabella. If nothing else, she wished she had her friend around to vent to.

To her relief though, it seemed Isabella had felt bad about lunchtime too. She greeted her roommate with a wide, apologetic smile as Cassie shut their door and slumped on to her bed.

'So. That was a little awkward earlier. I'm sorry, Cassie. I guess we just need to adapt to each other's new lifestyles now, move onwards and upwards, no?'

Cassie sighed. 'Definitely.'

'Well, to seal the meal once and for all, how about our

girls' night in? Smuggle in a bottle of champagne . . . And I'll get caviar, smoked salmon. Blinis! We can have a picnic. Listen to some music. I'll give you all the gossip from the non-Few. How about it?' Her eyes were bright with mischief, but underlain with anxiety.

'You're on.' Cassie felt her mood lift. 'Blinis are my favourite! You can get some here?'

'I can always get anything.' Isabella squeezed her arm. 'This will be good fun! Just you and me and my make-up case.'

Cassie's heart sank, and not just at the thought of leaving her face to Isabella's mercy. 'Wait, but you don't mean tonight though, right?'

'Yes, tonight! No time like the present, Cassie Bell.' Isabella grinned and began scrolling through her mobile phone contacts. 'I'll call my father's favourite hotel here, see if they can spare some supplies for their favourite client's daughter.'

'Oh, Isabella, I'm sorry.' Cassie could hardly bring herself to say it. 'I said I'd go to a . . . a Few party tonight.'

'*Again?*' Isabella couldn't disguise her disappointment. 'Where . . . ?'

'Another island. It's between here and the Asian side. I'm really sorry, Isabella. We'll take a rain check, though. Is that OK?'

'Of course.' There was something frosty about Isabella's tone.

'I mean, I'd invite you too, but . . .'

'It's Few Only.'

Cassie swallowed, feeling like dirt. 'They made that pretty clear. Or I'd have asked you when I first heard, obviously.'

'I understand. There are some times when the Few make the rest of us welcome, and others . . . well. I understand. I hope you have a lovely time.'

Cassie couldn't bear to hear that clipped tone in her friend's voice. 'Isabella, come on. I'm sure there's other stuff you want to do with me out of your hair for an evening. Then we can take the time to plan our night properly, make it really cool—'

'Uh, yes.' Quite abruptly, and to Cassie's astonishment, her friend's face had brightened, as though something had just occurred to her. 'What am I saying? You're right. Look, don't be sorry, Cassie. *I'm* sorry! That was so graceless of me. You are to go and have a good time.'

'Really?' Cassie blinked with shock.

'Really! It's OK, I could . . . I could use some time to myself. Honestly, I mean it! Go and have fun.'

'If you're sure . . .'

'Of course I am. Besides, a party means I can still work

on that make-up of yours, no?' Isabella grinned devilishly. 'Let's get you looking your best!'

Speaking of which . . . Cassie almost didn't dare ask. 'Isabella, I—'

'What? Oh, I know what it is. I know that look.' Isabella's smile became ever so slightly more forced.

'You know I wouldn't ask. It's just—'

'No, Cassie, of course, it's OK. Of course you need to feed. Don't worry. Really.' Isabella couldn't quite meet her eyes, she noticed. 'I insist. I told you, we want you looking your best.'

'Thanks, Isabella. I appreciate it.'

Isabella took a deep breath and brightened again. 'Besides, then you will *have* to submit to a makeover. Payback, yes?'

'Yeah. Payback,' Cassie mumbled, nodding but uncomfortable with the word. She owed her friend some of the control back after what she put her through, it was true. 'Isabella.' Cassie hugged her friend. 'You are a star. Incorrigible, but a star.'

CHAPTER TWELVE

The island had a different atmosphere to the Academy's – it felt somehow more free-and-easy, less formal – but it had the same dusky-scented beauty, and the small palace (Cassie had an inward giggle at the concept) shared the same splendid architecture and intricate decoration. Cassie stood at a stone balustrade, one hand resting on the warm gilded wood of an arch, champagne cocktail in the other. Across the silky pewter of the twilit Bosphorus she could see floodlit domes and minarets picked out against an indigo sky, and the cries of muezzin were clearly audible in the evening air. The loveliness and strange loneliness of it made her heart ache in her chest like the broken spirit of Estelle. Sometimes it was hard to tell which was which.

Behind her there was a hubbub of conversation, occasional squeals or guffaws, the bass throb of music. It was a good party, but it felt oppressively hot in that room with its magnificent vaulted ceilings and its rich dark fabrics. Cassie had slipped off Isabella's stilettos, and was enjoying the sensation of soft and expensive Turkish rug between her toes. She wished she could afford to buy one, but then where would she put it? The TV lounge at Cranlake Crescent? Grinning, she took another swallow of cocktail and felt it zing straight to her head.

Well, back to the fray . . .

She didn't bother to put the Manolos back on. She liked the barefoot feeling, and it wasn't as if she needed the extra height. The Few students were treating her with respect now, even the ones who didn't hold her in much affection; people were greeting her cheerfully and drawing her into their conversations. They were all rich, elegant, polished to within an inch of their privileged lives, yet their eyes seemed drawn to her like a magnet as she passed, and in more than a few of those gazes there was deference, and even a little fear. She liked being Few, she realised with a happy jolt . . .

A cut-glass voice sliced into her reverie. 'Oh look, if it isn't ding-dong Bell again. Nice frock. Where do you think she got it? Primark? Or just nicked?'

Cassie halted. Trust Sara to try and spike her evening. Turning, Cassie glared right into the sixth former's face as she stood by the bar next to Mikhail – the person to whom the girl was supposedly directing her comments. Sara's face twisted with distaste at Cassie's reaction, but she couldn't help flinching a little. Remembering, no doubt, how Cassie had dealt with her at a similar bar in Carnegie Hall that February . . .

Honestly, the girl was tragic. Did she really imagine that Cassie cared any more what she thought? Still, it was fun to watch the fear flit across her face, chasing out the hatred.

'All alone, Cassandra?' That was Mikhail, sidling closer to Sara, though Cassie couldn't tell if he was supporting the English girl or looking for safety in numbers. 'No date? Oh, that's right. Ranjit's turned all Harry Houdini on us and disappeared. Poor thing. Perhaps our prince is after a taste of the high life, having slummed it last term?' He arched an eyebrow at Sara pointedly.

Cassie drew back her lips to show her teeth. The light in the room was suddenly a little redder. 'Want to come out from Sara's skirts and say that again, Mikhail?'

'How dare you, you utter chav. Who do you think you—'

'Would you like to find out exactly who I am?' She let the red flood her eyes. Damn, she hadn't wanted to let them get to her. If the little dick hadn't brought Ranjit into it—

'Cassie! Hey!' An arm slipped round her waist, surprising her enough to let a little of the red drain from her vision.

'Oh, Richard,' drawled Sara. 'Trust you to lower yourself.'

'Well, we know he isn't fussy,' added Mikhail bitchily.

'And you should know, Mickey, my lad.' Richard gazed solemnly into Cassie's eyes, then looked back at the other two with an innocent smile. 'Doesn't Ms Bell just look set to stun? We ought to be careful, it could be dangerous just to look at her the wrong way.'

Sara took an involuntary step back. She looked furious at herself, but there was no hiding her instinctive nervousness.

Richard let it go, his small victory achieved. 'Please dance with me, Cassie. You're the best-looking girl in the room. Bar none.'

Cassie grinned. It wasn't just that she was glad of a diversion. Richard looked exceptionally good in a tux. And his eyes were alight with mischief, which couldn't help but make him even more attractive. 'Why, thank you, Richard. I'd be delighted.'

She didn't wait to watch the fury on the faces of Sara

and Mikhail, but turned and let Richard guide her to the cleared space where people were dancing.

'Hmm, bit of a smoochy one, isn't it?' she said dryly as she twined her arms round his neck.

'I'm not the one choosing the music,' he murmured. 'You looked like you needed an escape – a peaceable one, anyway. And you do look fantastic, I wasn't joking, so I thought I'd take my opportunity where I could get it.'

Cassie angled her head up to look at him, expecting the usual glint of wickedness in his eye, but it was missing. Instead he looked almost wistful.

A little taken aback, she glanced down at Isabella's scarlet dress. 'It's borrowed.'

'Who cares?'

'And anyone would look fantastic after Isabella's ministrations.' This was ridiculous; she felt quite flustered. 'You're just doing that charming thing again.'

'I can't help it. It's in the blood.'

Speaking of blood, she could feel his. She could feel it throbbing through his veins, feel the thud of his heart against her chest. It should have made her nervous, but she found she liked it. Almost involuntarily she nestled closer against him. After tensing a little with surprise, he relaxed and held her closer.

'Bugger,' he said softly in her ear as the music changed. 'I hate this song.'

'Good. Me too.' She drew back from him.

'Too fast for me anyway. I'd fall over my own feet.'

She laughed. 'Highly unlikely,' she shouted as the volume and the beat soared. 'I might pop out for some air, I'm roasting.' She hesitated. 'Care to join me?'

Outside, clutching new drinks for both of them, Richard leaned on the balustrade beside her and handed her a glass. Nervously he turned his own in his hands. Once again she noticed how strong they looked, the knuckles prominent, the sinews etched on his skin. Nice hands. Attractive hands.

'So, um.' He seemed to be casting around for safe conversational topics. 'What's going on with Ranjit?' He'd failed. 'I, uh, I haven't seen him around much lately. Are you—'

'No,' she interrupted. 'We're not. D'you know what, let's not talk about him right now.'

'You mean, you don't know where he's got to either? You haven't seen him?' He paused. 'You must be worried.'

'No,' she lied. The night was black velvet now, the stars glittering over the sea and the city. She didn't want to think about Ranjit, not at the moment. And Estelle was maintaining a low snarky bitching at the back of her brain, a moan about the inferiority of a mate. She wanted to drown her out. What business was it of hers? It wasn't as if she even regarded Richard as a 'mate', was it?

And yet, she was enjoying his closeness, more than she cared to admit. His arm was touching hers, and she didn't want to pull away. Actually she wanted to lean closer. Even as the thought occurred to her, she felt her breathing quicken. Weird. But it was hard to catch her breath, she realised, only because her heart was skipping and thudding in her ribcage.

Stunned, she turned her head, and found he was looking at her with an expression that suggested he was feeling something too. The same shock, the same intensity. Unable to pull her eyes away from his, Cassie took a deep breath and—

'Hey, you guys! Quit hiding!'

They both spun on their heels in unison, breaking the contact of their bodies. Richard cursed under his breath, a wry grin on his lips.

'Ayeesha! What's up?' Cassie covered her confusion with a grin. 'Where's Cormac? Off his face?'

Ayeesha mock-gasped and slapped Cassie's arm cheerfully. 'Nah, he's good. We're all planning a trip into town, check out some nightclubs. It's sociological research!'

'Sounds good to me.' Richard turned to Cassie with a casual tilt of his eyebrow.

'Mikhail said he was coming, unfortunately, but I'll make sure he behaves,' said Ayeesha with a glower in the direction of the snotty Russian boy. He didn't see it, being wrapped round Saski. 'I saw him and Sara trying to bait you earlier – nicely handled, by the way. I've already given him an earful about how he's been acting.'

'I'll bet you have!' Cassie laughed, then shook her head. 'Nothing to do with that, but you know what? I think I'll call it a night.'

'Really?' said Richard, with an edge of disappointment.

'Really.' She touched his hand and smiled. 'Nothing personal, seriously. It's not you and it's certainly not Mikhail. It's Isabella. I felt kind of guilty leaving her, she's understandably been finding things difficult lately, and I don't want to be out till all hours. If I head home and give her some gossip, hopefully she'll forgive me for not being around so much this term. And I *do* owe her for this dress.'

'Good point.' He leaned forward and kissed her cheek, his lips lingering a moment longer than was necessary, making her skin tingle.

Single and ready to tingle, Cassandra . . . Are you still trying to deny it?

Cassie blushed, ignoring Estelle as Richard continued. 'See you tomorrow, maybe?'

'Uh, sure. Go on, have fun. See you, guys. Oh, but Ayeesha?' She paused. 'Don't let him get into any trouble, will you?'

Ayeesha gave an unladylike bellow of laughter, then hooked her arm through Richard's and led him off. Cassie gazed after them wistfully, then shook herself. It would have been fun – maybe too much fun. But quite honestly she was glad of the break. She needed to have a good hard think about a few things.

'Hi, honey, I'm home!'

Cassie barged happily into the room they shared. She'd missed Isabella, she realised; a night out just wasn't the same without the wild-haired, wild-brained Argentinian. They had to get back on some kind of even keel. Isabella's was the friendship she valued most in the world, for heaven's sake.

For a fleeting second Isabella didn't seem to hear her. She was at her desk in the far corner, tousled head bent. 'It was great to see you,' she told her laptop softly.

Ah. She was engrossed in a webchat. As she raised her head, seeming to feel Cassie more than hear her, she snapped her head round swiftly and broke it off.

A click of the mouse closed the chat window.

'Hi!' There was a crimson tinge to Isabella's cheekbones.

'Hey!' Bouncing down on the bed closest to her friend, Cassie smiled. 'Who were you chatting to?'

'My mother. She says hi.' The crimson shade deepened.

'Oh! Your dad too?'

'Nope. I mean, yeah, I'm sure he sends his love as well.' Hurriedly Isabella closed the laptop.

'No, it was just, I thought I heard—' A male voice? A weirdly familiar one, at that. Cassie shook herself. Few hearing she might have, but she was more than a little tipsy. She could have been mistaken. Maybe . . .

But it was none of her business. And the important thing was getting back on solid ground with Isabella, not interrogating her.

'Have I got some gossip for *you*!' Cassie gave her roommate a broad grin.

'Good!' Isabella clapped her hands, her expression relaxing. 'That's the only reason I allowed you to go to the party! Now, just before you start, wait five – I got hold of that bottle of champagne . . .'

CHAPTER THIRTEEN

'Ouch. Ouch, ouch, ouch.' Cassie rolled over on to her face, dragging a pillow over her head to shut out the morning light. The distant wail of muezzin and the soft cooing of a dove echoed painfully in her head. 'Never again,' she moaned into the mattress.

It was long minutes before she could ease herself into the light of a new day. Blinking groggily at the other bed, she saw her roommate was still fast asleep and snoring. The sleep of the just, Cassie thought, rolling her eyes in envy. Oh, blimey, even that hurt . . .

Stumbling to the glass-walled shower she turned it on hard and hot. That felt better. The pink-brown dove was at the bathroom window now, chirping its head off, but it sounded more soothing now than painful. Cassie closed her eyes blissfully, letting hot needles of water wash away her headache.

Then, suddenly, a scream pierced through the dull fuzz in her head. A blood-chilling, desperate howl.

The dove flapped away in fright. Cassie slammed the water off and stood for a moment, befuddled, her heart slamming against her chest with the shock. Then, snatching up a towel, she ran back into the bedroom.

She sighed with relief. Not Isabella. The Argentinian girl still snored peacefully, face obscured by her mess of mahogany hair. Cassie hopped from foot to foot, quickly towelling herself dry, and wondered if she'd imagined the scream.

Then it came again, shattering the morning quiet. It came from outside in the corridor, but echoing through the open shutters of the courtyard. Hauling on jeans and dragging a T-shirt over her head, Cassie flung open the door and ran in the direction of the screaming.

By the time she'd found the source, the hysterical screams had turned to wailing sobs. Clustered around a crying girl was a group of other students, all of them in various states of undress and bemusement. The girl was crouched on the ground, but then she suddenly leaped to her feet, flailing, batting them away.

Cassie darted forward instinctively, seizing her arms. 'Sh! Calm down, what is it? What's wrong? Hey!'

The girl fought her for a few seconds, but then seemed

to recognise Cassie almost at the same moment as Cassie recognised her.

God, it was Saski! The new third-year Few girl. Cassie drew back, staring at her but still holding fast to her arms. The girl she'd last seen giggling in Mikhail's embrace, heading down to the launch jetty with him to go and 'research' nightclubs.

'Quiet,' she whispered to the sobbing girl. 'Calm down!' Turning to the ogling hordes, she saw there were no other Few. Ah, no wonder they were brimming with such hungry curiosity. With a deep breath, Cassie drew herself taller and reluctantly mustered her Few authority.

'All right, end of show. Go on, get out of here. Can't you see she's upset?' She glared at the more reluctant ones. 'Seriously, this is nothing to do with you. We'll sort it out.' They seemed to understand what she meant by 'we', even if Cassie wasn't exactly sure what the Few would be able to do about whatever it was that was upsetting Saski so much. Still, it was enough to send them packing; the crowd dispersed, muttering, back to their rooms.

Ignoring the bitchy comments whispered in her direction, Cassie helped the hysterical girl to her feet and pulled her towards an alcove. At least all this had done for her hangover.

'What is it, for heaven's sake? *Hey!* Settle down, Saski, and I'll try and help you!'

The girl took gulps of air, sniffing and rubbing her eyes, and at last the juddering of her body calmed down enough for her to say something intelligible.

'M-Mikhail!'

'Mikhail?' Cassie narrowed her eyes. 'What about him? What's he done to you?'

'*Nothing!* He'll never do anything again! Oh my God. Oh my God. He's *dead!*'

Cassie's breath stopped in her throat. Arms tightening around the girl, she felt her heart thrash. 'What? Don't be silly. You had a nightmare—'

'*NO!* He's dead. He's dead!' The girl's voice was nothing more than a whisper now as she gasped in sobbing lungfuls of air. Cassie stroked her head and tried to calm her. At last she managed to murmur, 'I went to find him in his room this morning. But just as I got there, some p-police arrived and . . . H-his roommate's in with Sir Alric right now.'

There was no more sense from Saski, as the tears returned with a vengeance. Cassie was aware of teachers gathering, of the silent figure of the porter Marat in the background, and the girl was eventually prised away from her and taken away by Madame Lefevre, who could do hugging and comforting a lot more efficiently than Cassie.

Cassie turned on Chelnikov, stunned. 'Is it true? Mikhail's dead?'

The science master's stony blue gaze was unchanged. 'You'll have to talk to Sir Alric about that. We're not at liberty to discuss the matter. Now, Miss Bell, I suggest you too return to your room.'

Cassie took a breath to argue, but stopped herself; there was nothing else for it. What would be the use in trying to pull Few rank again at this point? Nodding, she did as she was told, her mind spinning. By the time she shut the heavy door to her room, leaned against it and breathed out a shaky sigh, Isabella was awake, and demanding to know what all the commotion had been about.

'He's *what*?' Her roommate's voice trembled.

'Dead,' said Cassie, swallowing hard. 'So Saski said.'

'That's ridiculous. No. That's crazy.'

Cassie shook her head, then rubbed the bridge of her nose. 'Apparently not. Some of the teachers seem to know about it. This is . . . . this is unbelievable.'

'*Beyond* unbelievable. Cassie, didn't Saski explain any more?'

'She couldn't, she's hysterical.' Cassie could feel herself heading that way herself. If Mikhail was dead, and Yusuf was missing, then Ranjit . . . Then Ranjit— 'No,' she muttered, half to herself. 'No, he's fine. He always is.'

Neither of them bothered with make-up. She and Isabella were down in the dining room for breakfast within ten minutes, together with what seemed like the rest of the school, loud with excitement and horror.

'It's the curse. That's what it is.'

'I'm going to have to call my parents. They'll be flipping out if they hear.'

'Lessons are cancelled. *As usual.* Finally some time to get a bit of shopping done . . .'

'*Torquil!*'

'Bloody hell, have you heard . . . ?'

'I never liked him, but how awful. Poor Saski.'

'. . . Curse, I'm telling you. The Darke Academy curse.'

Cassie tried to drown out all the speculating as she and Isabella walked over and sat down with Alice.

'Have you heard what happened?' Isabella said, gripping Alice's hand comfortingly. Alice looked shakier than some of the others – but then she'd experienced her own Few roommate dying in mysterious and nasty circumstances not so long ago. Luckily she didn't know that Keiko had died at Cassie's hands, in self-defence while the unhinged Japanese girl was trying to stab *her* to death . . . Cassie shuddered, trying not to think about it, in case the guilt showed in her face.

'Yes. Well, only the basics. They haven't really told us anything.'

Feeling a hand on her shoulder, Cassie turned to her left: India. The Few girl looked subdued, and almost frightened. She got up and let India draw her aside, trying to ignore Isabella's pointed look. She needed to get all the information she could; all of it could help. Help towards finding him.

'They found him at five o'clock this morning,' India murmured, as they sat down on a bench in the courtyard. 'Down at the Golden Horn, by the harbour. God knows how he'd got there. We got separated from him in Beyoglu, but we weren't worried. We were more concerned about getting Saski home, cos she was too pissed to stand. It never occurred to us that Mikhail . . .'

'No,' said Cassie. 'It wouldn't. He was one of . . . one of us. God, what on earth happened?'

'Nobody knows. They're keeping the details very hush-hush.'

I'll bet they are, thought Cassie grimly. It had been the same with Keiko, after all. She had a sudden, vivid mental picture of Marat, down in the shadows below her, flinging a white sheet over Keiko's desiccated remains. And before that, hadn't they covered up the dreadful killing of Jess?

Why, Sir Alric would be greasing palms in the Istanbul police force at this very moment . . .

Someone appeared behind her and India, leaning forward between them, clasping his hands nervously. Antonio, a fifth-year Few boy. Not one she knew well, but relatively friendly.

'Emergency meeting after breakfast, Cassie, India. Can you be there? It's important.'

'It certainly is.' Cassie gave him a wry look, then glanced at India. 'Of course I'll be there.'

'And so will I,' added India.

'Good. The common room, ten o'clock. See you there.' He stood up and headed in the direction of two more Few members.

He seemed antsy and quick. He must have got round them all, because by the time Cassie arrived at the common room they were all there. No one seemed to be missing – except for Mikhail, of course.

And Yusuf, she thought with a shudder of unease.

And Ranjit . . .

She felt a friendly presence at her shoulder, and didn't have to turn to know it was Richard. She sighed. Despite the circumstances, she couldn't help feeling a small sense of relief at having him there.

'Hi,' she murmured.

'Cassie.' His voice was sombre.

'What happened after I left, Richard?' She gave him a sidelong glance. 'Did you see anything?'

'No.' He touched her arm, and a quiver ran up it. 'I left early. It wasn't any fun without you there.' He bit his lip, his eyebrow arching ever so slightly.

Cassie smiled.

The hubbub in the room died as one of the older Few, Vassily, rattled a silver fork against his glass. 'Is everyone here?'

Ayeesha glanced around the room, counting. 'Yes.'

'Right. We can safely say we have two Few missing, and now one dead. It doesn't look good for us.'

There was a general murmur of worried assent.

'I think we're agreed on one thing: we're vulnerable. And this is not something that we are used to.' Vassily took a deep breath. 'This has to stop.'

'But how?' someone interjected from the back of the group.

That question alone was asking for more trouble. Everyone, of course, had their own theories, their own answers, and fear had made them voluble. The room erupted.

Cassie kept quiet, listening hard to the suggestions and the arguments, letting the shouted questions batter her ears. She kept her mouth shut partly because they didn't seem to be getting anywhere, but mostly because one name kept cropping up with alarming frequency.

'What about Cassie?' a voice chimed once more.

Ayeesha spoke up. 'I agree. Cassie, there's no denying that you handle Darke better than most of us – he has a special, ah . . . concern when it comes to you. It could be the in we need, huh?'

Gazes flicked towards Cassie, with nervousness and respect.

'Mm, *and* she has a personal interest in . . . well. You know who,' someone murmured, to some snickers.

'Yes. I think she should represent us,' someone else said.

'Oh, hold on a minute.' That was Sara's sneer. 'You're not telling me that *psycho Scholarship* is going to represent us? Not in my name, I assure you.'

'Oh shut up, Sara,' snapped India.

'Cassie's the obvious delegate,' said Cormac. 'Sir Alric likes her.'

'Sir Alric's losing his marbles.'

'It's a bloody no-brainer,' shouted another student on the other side of the room. 'With Ranjit gone, she's the most powerful one of us, no contest. She's the best candidate for the job.'

Vassily rapped on the glass again. 'Does the proposed delegate have anything to say about it herself?'

All eyes turned her way. Cassie took a deep breath.

'You want me to talk to Sir Alric? Fine, I'll talk to him. But you're going to have to tell me what you want me to say.'

'So you're willing?' Vassily raised an eyebrow, and then glanced round the room. 'Any objections?' As Sara opened her mouth again he added, 'Any *rational* objections?'

She shut it again, looking venomous. So did a few others around her, but most of the Few were nodding approvingly.

Yes, my dear! We have them all in the palm of our hands now! You are their chosen one!

'Thank you, Cassie,' Vassily was saying, as Cassie clenched her jaw. 'It's nothing complicated. As we were saying: Mikhail's dead. Ranjit and Yusuf are missing. They had nothing in common but their gender – and the fact that they're all Few. So unless there's some mad feminist killer out there, I think it's pretty obvious what the connection might be.'

'And you want me to ask what, exactly?' insisted Cassie.

He paused, glancing at some of the others. 'What Sir Alric knows.'

'What he *doesn't* know,' added Antonio.

'How soon he knew it.' That was India. 'And why we know nothing yet. Why we've been kept in . . .' she paused and smiled bleakly, '. . . the dark.'

Vassily turned back to Cassie. 'You get the gist.'

She nodded. Since the news of Mikhail's death, her vague worries about Ranjit had coalesced into something ten times more frightening. Whether it was over between them or not, she needed to do something concrete, and she needed to do it *now*.

'I hope she's not going to be emotional about this,' snapped Sara.

'She's an official delegate of the Few,' said Vassily, who Cassie was beginning to realise couldn't stand Sara. 'I think we can rely on her not to be *emotional*.' He gave Cassie a curt look, and she nodded once.

'Then choose her sidesmen,' he said, slumping back into his chair. 'We'll do this the correct way. Officially. And then Sir Alric Darke will tell us what he knows.'

CHAPTER FOURTEEN

'Cassandra Bell.' Sir Alric Darke stood quite formally as his secretary opened the door to the delegation. A smile of satisfaction twitched his mouth. She walked into the room, giving a last glance at her 'sidesmen'. Ayeesha was solemn, but Richard gave her a reassuring nod as Sir Alric dismissed them and the door was closed.

'So, Cassie. Official delegate of the Few, no less. In two terms.'

'I don't really care about that. Not right now.'

She swept the room with her gaze. There was something odd about it since last time. Sir Alric himself, for a start. He looked almost dishevelled – well, by his standards at least. His hair was rumpled from having his long fingers run through it, and his tie was slightly loosened. She couldn't even be sure he'd shaved today. As for the room, it was strewn with papers, folders, books. Cassie frowned. And there was something different, something missing. She couldn't put her finger on it, but something . . .

He must have noticed her curiosity, because he looked quite shifty and displeased all of a sudden. 'There's a little disorder here; I seem to have misplaced a file. Shall we go out to the greenhouse?'

As ever, it wasn't really a request, so she followed him. He didn't even give his young orchids a glance as he passed them; now that was unusual. Curiouser and curiouser . . .

'So.' Sir Alric stood silhouetted against one of the glass walls lined with creeping vines, and folded his arms. 'Please feel free to present your request.'

Cassie cleared her throat, thinking she should play along with his formalities. 'I – *we*, the Few – want to be made privy to any information you have about Mikhail's death. About Yusuf's disappearance, and . . . and Ranjit's.' She took a deep breath, angry that she'd stumbled over the name. 'Because the Few believe that sleeping dogs shouldn't be left to lie any longer. This is directly affecting us, and we have a right to know.' When she was finished, she was a little surprised herself at how severe she had managed to sound.

Sir Alric didn't answer immediately. He nodded slowly,

deliberately, and then smoothed a ruffled hair back into place, before folding his arms again and finally meeting her eye.

'I grant you, Cassie, the situation is unusual in that there does seem to be a connection between these disappearances. But as you've told me yourself, Ranjit Singh keeps very much to his own schedule.' He paused. 'And as I've already asked you, I want you to let me know if he gets in touch.'

'What makes you think he'd get in touch with me?'

'Come along, Cassie. Let's not play games.'

She bristled. Here he was, quite literally in a glass house, and he was going to throw stones at her?

'You seem very certain everything's all right with him.'

'Nothing is certain,' he replied, his eyes stormy, severe. 'But we both know that of anyone, you are the most likely person he would contact. It's important that anything pertaining to this matter is brought to my attention straight away.' He raised an eyebrow pointedly.

Cassie clenched her jaw before taking a breath and speaking again, her voice low as she struggled to control the heat building behind her eyes. 'If you're trying to suggest I'm keeping something from you, you're dead wrong. There have been no secret rendezvous, no clandestine meetings so you can stop suggesting that—'

'Not even with a certain Mr Johnson?'

Cassie froze. 'What?'

'Have you been in contact with Jake Johnson?'

The question came out of left field, catching her completely off guard. It was a moment before she could catch her breath to answer. Even then she didn't cover herself with glory.

'Eh?' she said, shaking her head in frustration, then jumping as Estelle's voice echoed inside her head.

The American boy! We should never have let him get out of our sight!

Sir Alric's brow was furrowed, and he was watching her very closely. Cassie composed herself before she spoke again.

'I haven't seen Jake since last term. Why would I? He hates me. He wouldn't send me so much as a postcard.'

'Really?'

'Really. I have absolutely no reason to lie. I haven't heard from him. And he definitely has good reason to hate me, as I'm sure you're aware. I doubt I'll ever see him again.' In a mutter she added, 'I'll be spending my life making that up to Isabella.'

His gaze remained unrelenting, but he nodded slowly. 'So you're unaware that Jake Johnson flew into Istanbul several days ago.'

She didn't think she'd ever been so comprehensively gobsmacked. She couldn't think of a single thing to say, except – again – 'What?'

'He's in Istanbul, Cassie.'

'*Where?*'

He gave an elegant shrug. 'I don't know, exactly. We haven't been able to track him down. He's disappeared from view, and now he's lying low. I've been expecting him to surface, and up until now I've seen no reason to . . . make anyone else aware.' He paused, and raised an arched eyebrow. 'Why do you think he'd come here, Cassie?'

'I . . . don't know. He's . . . he still wants to get to the bottom of Jessica's death, of course.' She tried to be cool, but found she was trembling. 'That's natural enough.'

'Yes.' Sir Alric nodded. 'Indeed. Very natural.'

She swallowed hard. 'Don't you believe me?'

'Yes, Cassie, I do. I think it's clear you haven't heard from him. And I don't think you need to worry about Jake in particular. He isn't capable of harming a member of the Few, in any case.'

The line of sweat prickling her hairline must be obvious to him. She was certain he knew that she couldn't speak because she didn't trust her voice.

The Knife. The supernatural, strangely powerful Knife.

Jake had it. That could harm the Few, all right. She'd seen it done. She remembered all that was left of Keiko: a smear of dried Keiko-shaped dust on a marble floor in Paris.

She cleared her throat. 'You still haven't told me about Mikhail. And . . . the other two. What you know.'

Again he lifted his shoulders gently. 'That's because I know very little, Cassie. Possibly even less than you do.'

She eyed him closely. 'If you say so,' she said, barely concealing her suspicion. Sir Alric ignored her.

'Now, a word about your new . . . status.'

She lifted her chin. 'Go on.'

'I'm pleased you have come so far among the Few in so short a time. Nevertheless, do not get complacent. As you are more than aware, you are special, even for a Few member.' Gently he touched the black petal of one of the propagated orchids pointedly. 'Like I told you before. You are unique, but that means others will be watching. And people could jump to conclusions about . . . unique situations. Do you understand?'

'Are you trying to say someone could accuse *me* of having something to do with this?'

Sir Alric fixed her with a severe glare. 'I'm saying that I think you should take last term's reprieve with the Council seriously.'

There was little more Cassie could say to that. She nodded, and walked back through his office with all the dignity she could muster. Darke's secretary opened the door, and let it swing shut with a soft *clunk* behind her. And until she was back in the corridors of the Academy, she felt his granite eyes boring into her spine.

CHAPTER FIFTEEN

'Nothing. He didn't tell me *anything*.' She was still fizzing with fury and confusion, and the rest of the Few didn't seem too upbeat either. '

'I knew she'd be useless,' murmured Sara to the girl at her side.

The others ignored that, and so did Cassie. She'd never seen the elite Few so restless, so unsure of themselves, so . . . *scared*.

'Is someone out to get us?' Cormac finally voiced what they were all thinking.

'Looks that way, doesn't it?' said Vassily. 'And it looks as if we can't expect any help from Darke.'

Cassie clamped her mouth shut, resolving to say nothing more. She'd done her bit: let the rest of them work it out from here. She had other things to think about.

Like Jake Johnson being in Istanbul . . .

Did Isabella know? And if she did, why would she hide it from Cassie?

Why would she hide it? Unless Isabella knew something. Unless Jake had something to do with . . .

. . . oh, God . . .

Cassie felt sick. If it had been an option she'd have bolted from the room and straight to the toilets, but that would attract too much attention and way too many questions. There must be an explanation. But how could she expect Isabella to explain anything to her, let alone something as sensitive as this? They'd been growing more and more like strangers since they'd stepped off the *Mistral Dancer*.

But still, they were *friends*, weren't they? They'd be friends for ever. Or at least that was what she used to think. All Cassie could think now was how much needed fixing in their relationship. She'd hardly been the greatest friend to Isabella: disdaining her for the company of the Few, treating her like a second-class citizen. And yet she'd had to, and that was Isabella's fault too, for kind of seeming to resent Cassie's new status, and being so stand-offish with the other Few . . .

Her head whirled. All she knew was what a bloody mess this was. Besides, she didn't even know for sure that

Isabella *did* know about Jake. And if she didn't – well, Cassie wasn't going to be the one to tell her.

It was just that she couldn't help remembering that moment when she'd come back to their room. A male voice on the webchat. Isabella so absorbed she didn't even hear Cassie come in. The look on her face when she finally did see her. And Isabella's recent, magical mood change . . .

A voice said her name. Starting, coming back to the present, she saw that the Few were all standing up, talking in low voices, leaving in small solemn groups.

'Cassie,' said Richard again.

'Sorry.' She shook herself. 'I was miles away.'

'I noticed. I'm not surprised. I wish we could go for a drink. That's the trouble about being stuck on this bloody island, isn't it?'

She rubbed her forehead, laughing shakily. 'I hadn't thought of it like that, but you're dead right. I suppose it's deliberate.'

'Yeah. I was thinking that. The bastard.' He grinned, then grew serious. 'He gave you a bad time, Darke, did he?'

'It's not that. He was perfectly polite and pleasant, as usual. But just no damn use at all. And I'm just, um . . . confused.' She sighed. 'And worried.'

Richard's eyebrows knitted together with concern. 'Well, look, there's half a bottle of red left from the party. Why don't we grab it and take it down to the beach?'

'I don't think—'

'Listen, Cassie.' He lowered his voice as they left the common room and he closed the door. They were last out. 'If it's about last night, I'm sorry – I mean, I don't want you to think— I promised I wouldn't give you any hassle. And I didn't mean to. You just . . . you look like you could use someone to talk to.'

She shook her head violently. 'No. It isn't that. Honestly.'

'You're sure?' He sounded so uncertain she put a hand on his arm and smiled.

'Positive. And actually I *would* like a walk on the beach, but I think I should clear my head rather than make it fuzzier.' She suppressed the corners of her mouth from turning up at Richard's slightly disappointed look. 'D'you reckon you could lay your mitts on some cold Coke?'

'Your wish?' he grinned, reopening the common room door behind him, then bowing deeply before disappearing inside. 'My compulsion.'

They didn't walk, as it turned out. Cassie was so tired, all she could do was perch on a rock and drink thirstily from the chilled litre of Coke that Richard had snaffled from the common room. Tiny waves lapped idly against the small crescent beach, edged with phosphorescence in the starlight. She could smell the flowers in the garden, drifting smoke and traffic fumes from the city, and that gentle, ever-present Bosphorus breeze. Something small rustled in the undergrowth at the edge of the beach: a cat, maybe. Floodlit spires and domes glowed in a pale line where the city lay across the glossy water.

She needed this. Some peace, just for a moment, something undemanding. She tilted the bottle to her lips once more.

Richard lay flat on the rock beside her, hands folded on his stomach, gazing up into the sky. He seemed to be going to great lengths to avoid touching her. So it was funny that she felt more comfortable in his company than she had in anyone else's for what seemed like a very long time.

She'd always sort of got on with him, she thought, even when she hadn't liked him very much. It wasn't just the charm, it was something else . . . his vulnerability, maybe? Or just his sheer animal attractiveness; that might well have something to do with it. Closing her eyes, she smiled to herself in the darkness. Over the last year she'd fallen for him, been let down by him, fallen for him again, then been betrayed in the most appalling way when he'd tricked her into being initiated in the Few ceremony. And yet he'd somehow managed to redeem himself yet again. He was unbelievably easy to be with, and that was something she could appreciate more and more as her life grew increasingly complicated. Being with Richard wasn't like the constant passion and fear and lust that went with . . . with some people's company. Or lack of it. It was somehow safe. Comfortable. But not without its frissons. Very, very nice, in fact.

Cassie was almost sleepy now. She'd almost managed to empty her mind of all the escalating worries, just for a moment. The frothy little waves hissed and receded on the sand, hypnotic in their rhythm. There was nothing she could do about it all right now – about Jake, what he might be doing in Istanbul, what Isabella might be keeping from her, where Ranjit might be or . . . or what might have happened to him.

'Cassie?'

'M-hmm?' She wondered idly if Richard was about to hit on her. She decided, on balance, that she didn't mind too much if he did.

But he didn't move. He sat up, clasped his hands tighter, as if he was praying, and said, 'There's something I've been wanting to tell you.'

Cassie set the Coke bottle down in a patch of sand, wiggling it till it stood up straight. Turning her head, she watched his face. It was still focused on the night sky. 'That sounds ominous.'

He gave a funny little shrug. 'It's certainly important.'

She bit her upper lip, her heart suddenly thudding faster. 'Richard. Is this about Mikhail or . . . or Ranjit? The disappearances?'

'Hell, no. Though some of the superstitious twits back there might think it was all part of the same curse.'

'There isn't a curse,' she scoffed. 'There's just some seriously twisted people around this place, that's all.'

'I couldn't agree more. Still . . .'

'Go on. You wanted to tell me something.' She focused very intently on his face. She wanted to see every expression that crossed it, to scout for signs of deceit or double-cross, but she found she also just liked looking at it. Well, he was Few. Of course he had a beautiful face. Mind you, Sara was Few, and she didn't like looking at *her* for extended periods.

'It's about the Academy.' He broke into her thoughts. 'Before you came. About what happened. You know? All that, uh, trouble with Jess. It was a very screwed-up time for the school, back then. A bit like now, in fact.'

'Go on.' She held her breath, still watching him. Her

pulse remained fast and strong in her throat.

'There's something I want— No.' Richard turned his head to stare at her. 'There's something I *need* to tell you.'

His gaze, now that it met hers, was incredibly intense. For a fleeting instant Cassie was scared to keep looking at him, scared to know what he wanted to tell her. It was going to be too much truth: she could see it in his agonised stare. So she slewed her eyes away, out beyond the rock, out to the edge of the black sea and the log that rolled in the waves, sucked out and tossed back in.

'It's about what happened in Cambodia.'

'Richard . . .'

'Please. Let me tell you what happened. I need to tell you.'

'Richard?' Cassie leaped to her feet, took a step forward and then stopped. She was paralysed, but not by what he was saying. She felt every muscle in her body tense as she watched that log, rolled by the gentle tide. It flopped in the shallow surf, and once more was dragged back by the tide. Rolled, and flopped again.

Logs didn't flop.

It wasn't a log.

Cassie gave a strangled cry, and jumped down from the rock. She heard Richard running too, but he wasn't shouting after her. He must have seen what she'd seen. When she reached the water's edge he was right beside her.

'Oh God,' he whispered.

Together they stared at it, sucked out once more into deeper water by the turning tide. A limp arm, and a featureless head, and wasted legs.

A corpse.

CHAPTER SIXTEEN

Cassie splashed out into the water, Richard close behind, both of them snatching helplessly at the darkness. It was as if the waves taunted them, gentle as they were. With a whimper Cassie grabbed for what might have been the remains of a sleeve – or perhaps skin – only to lose her hold and see the corpse sucked back out by the undertow.

She gave a furious sob of frustration as Richard put an arm round her and pulled her back.

'We'll call someone,' he shouted, his phone already in his free hand. 'We'll get help.'

'Sod help!' she screamed. 'It's too sodding late for *help*!'

With that she jerked free of his hold, clenched her fists. It couldn't be him, *couldn't*. Not when she'd just been remembering how alive he'd been, their bodies crackling with passion. *It couldn't be Ranjit.*

Remembering Carnegie Hall, summoning all her power, she concentrated it on a point between her and the corpse.

Richard, watching, stepped warily back, his phone at his ear. She ignored him, feeling the power of the spirit extend beyond her as it had done before. Easy. She reached out with it, invisible tangling cords of thought and force coiling round the elusive body. And the power intensified.

The little waves were no match for her, though their phosphorescence was scarlet now in her field of vision. The power was fully outside her now, the sea air crackling with it. She took a breath, drew the corpse towards her using the invisible force. The body came easily to shore, and she hauled it out of the water to collapse like an emptied sack on the pebbles and sand.

'Bloody hell,' whispered Richard, snapping his phone shut.

She closed her eyes, staggering, not weak but very dizzy. In a second he was beside her, gripping her arm to steady her, then helping her drag the grotesque thing well clear of the water. Grains of sand clung to it, and the dead weight of it furrowed a deep channel in the beach until they could move it no further. They let it slump, face down. Or so she assumed, Cassie thought, feeling the beginnings of hysteria. She whimpered again, drained by the effort, terrified of seeing whatever face the thing had left.

Richard's arms were tight around her, turning her away from the sight. But his shocked whisper was in her ear, too. 'How the hell did you do that?'

He wasn't the only one asking. Slowly she became aware of voices behind her, people spilling out from the school – all Few, since they were so close to the common room.

'Jesus.'

'What is it?'

'You mean, who is it . . .'

'Did you see what she—'

'How on earth—'

'It's like frigging Carnegie Hall all over again. What's she done?'

'What *has* she done?'

'My *God* . . .'

If they didn't shut up she was going to kill one of them. Tears stinging her eyes, Cassie crammed her hands over her ears, shutting out the hubbub, forcing even Richard away.

Then she thought: Why am I just standing here!

Before Richard could grab her, she'd bolted back to the

drowned corpse, falling to her knees beside it. With a high-pitched intake of breath, then a shriek of revulsion, she reached out and shoved the thing on to its back.

No. No, she was being stupid. Of course there was no reviving it. There was no face to receive the kiss of life; nothing left but a vague semi-human shadow of a person. Tears rolled down her face and on to what had been living flesh. Grief, she knew it. Grief, but relief as well. Because as unrecognisable as this thing was, it was not Ranjit.

Unless Ranjit Singh was wearing Yusuf Ahmed's pendant.

Cassie was reaching out to touch the distinctive gold shark tooth with a trembling finger when she heard the commanding shout.

'Don't touch him. Don't touch anything.'

She turned, her vision still blurred by both power and tears, and saw a familiar figure approaching through a crowd of students – a crowd that parted for him without a word.

'Move away, Cassie,' said Sir Alric Darke.

Behind him she could make out the familiar figure of Marat, silent and squat as ever. And just as she'd seen him once before, he held a sheet draped over his arm. A shroud, all ready. As if he'd been waiting for this moment.

Sir Alric gazed down at the remains of Yusuf with an unreadable expression. What could she read there? wondered Cassie. Pity? Grief? Anger?

Nothing. Nothing at all. Except perhaps perplexity.

'There's nothing more to see here,' said Sir Alric abruptly, turning to face the gaggle of watchers. 'I've called the authorities. Return to your rooms. And for God's sake, try for once to refrain from pointless gossip. You'll get more information as soon as I do.'

The crowd dissipated, but there was no shaking the air of dread and thrill that hung over the beach. Cassie remained where she was, staring down at Yusuf until Marat stepped briskly past her and flung the sheet over the corpse.

The careless gesture reminded her so much of what had happened with Keiko it was painful. A terrible shard of remorse went through her, and she snapped her gaze up to Sir Alric, who remained stony-faced.

'What happened to him?' whispered Cassie.

'I don't know any more than you do.'

'Don't you?' She glowered at him.

'No, Miss Bell, I do not. Now Richard, Cassie, I suggest you take some time to rest; you are of course shocked. I will see you both in my office tomorrow morning. First thing, if you please. And, Miss Bell?'

She matched his steely stare.

'Be careful where you show off those powers,' he growled, and strode away from them, back to the faithful Marat and that pathetic, sodden cadaver.

Richard took her hand as they climbed across the rocks and up towards the Academy. She didn't mind. It didn't feel like a try-on, just comforting.

'I'm really sorry, Cassie,' he said in a low voice. 'You have the most god-awful luck. You shouldn't have had to see that.'

'Somebody had to.'

'I'm glad—' He hesitated and squeezed her hand. 'I'm glad it wasn't Ranjit.'

She gave a gasping laugh. 'Me too.' Then she sobered, very swiftly. 'But poor Yusuf. God, I wonder what happened to him?'

'Too much to drink. Slipped and fell in.'

'Oh come on, Richard.' She shot him a glance. 'You saw him as well as I did. He didn't drown.'

Richard was silent till they were in the corridors of the Academy, and then he kept his voice very low. 'He might have, Cassie. Water can do awful things. Fish. You know?'

'Richard, the boy was like— God, I can't even say it.' Like a dried piece of meat left soaking in water? Like a used teabag, all shrivelled up? She rubbed her hands violently against her jeans, trying to erase the tactile memory. Like a wet mummy. That was it. That body had been desiccated. Soaked again afterwards, making it gummy as mucus, but sucked dry first. Cassie came to a halt with a sound of revulsion, put her hands over her head and shut her eyes tight. 'Richard, get real.'

'All right,' he sighed. 'I'll walk you back to your room.'

'No it's fi—' She hesitated. 'Actually, yes, OK. That would be great. Thanks.'

He took her hand again, and kept it firmly in his. 'You don't have to put up a front with me, Cassie,' he said gently. 'You're scared, and that's understandable. More than understandable.'

'Yeah.'

'I am too.' He turned at her door and pulled her into his arms for a tight hug. She could feel his breath against her neck, and it felt hugely comforting, and oddly electric. 'Night, Cassie,' he whispered.

'Night, Richard.'

She watched him walk away, a small thrill of lust giving way as the sense of dread reasserted itself. For a moment she was tempted to run after him and confide, but that would be stupid. Richard didn't know what had happened to Keiko. And she just couldn't tell him about Jake being in Istanbul.

So she could hardly tell him that Keiko's corpse had looked just like Yusuf's. Right after Cassie had thrust in the Knife. The Knife that Jake still had.

CHAPTER SEVENTEEN

Cassie paused with her hand on the door of her shared room and pressed her forehead to the warm wood. She was dreading the next few minutes, but this had gone beyond tact, beyond discretion, perhaps beyond loyalty. She had to talk to Isabella about what was going on.

Taking a deep breath, easing the door open and then shutting it firmly behind her, she stared at her roommate, feeling for the first time as if she barely knew her.

Looking up, Isabella smiled. 'Hey! I was beginning to wonder where you were. Common room again?' she added, an eyebrow raised sarcastically.

Cassie looked at her roommate, confused. 'Well yeah I was, earlier. But it was hardly a social occasion. We're trying to figure out what's going on. As you might imagine, everyone's a bit on edge.'

'Yes, I can imagine. I feel bad, this must all be so

difficult for you,' Isabella said, then paused, smiling awkwardly as Cassie noticed the glitzy shopping bags by Isabella's bed. 'Yes, uh, we went shopping today. But I got you something too . . . Look. I thought it might cheer you up, just a little?' Isabella reached down and rustled one of the bags. 'Do you like it? It's silk.' She handed Cassie a beautifully woven scarf, but Cassie remained silent. The only thing she could think was: was Isabella feeling guilty? Was this actually designed to make *her* feel better?

'We went to Hussein Chalayan, and Umit Unal.' Isabella continued babbling. 'Honestly, Cassie. If you think I'm bad with a gold card, you should see Alice . . .'

Cassie stared at her cheerful roommate, baffled. Then she realised. 'Isabella. You haven't heard? I thought it would have spread like lightning.'

'Heard what?' Isabella was drawing something velvety and expensive out of one of the bags.

'Isabella.' Cassie sat down on the bed, clutching the fistfuls of bedspread to stop her hands shaking. 'Yusuf's dead.'

Isabella froze. '*What?* Cassie . . . how could you let me go on . . . ? Oh my God. How?'

'He was found . . .' Cassie took a breath. 'I mean, I found him. Down by the shore. Richard and me.'

'But. That's . . . that's awful!'

'You haven't been out of the room this evening? Didn't you hear all the commotion?'

'No, I . . . I've been busy – homework . . .'

The silence between them was electric. Cassie narrowed her eyes, watching Isabella closely. But it seemed Isabella was no more going to lower her gaze than she was. There was no way around it. She was just going to have to come right out and ask. She took a breath, and closed her eyes briefly.

'Isabella, has Jake been in touch with you? I need to know.'

The muscles of her friend's face tightened, and she hesitated. 'Why?'

'Because he's in Istanbul.'

She watched Isabella's rigid face, desperate for some sign that it was a shock. That she hadn't known. The girl could be pleased, indignant, hysterical with delight, she didn't care. Just so long as she *hadn't known* . . .

But Isabella just stuffed the dress she had been pulling out back into its expensive-looking bag, before speaking again in a clipped tone. 'What makes you think he's in Istanbul?'

Cassie clenched her jaw. 'Sir Alric had news. Jake's been seen.'

'Oh.' Isabella turned away to check her reflection, quite

176

unnecessarily, in the gilded mirror. Cassie could see worry and panic flicker into her roommate's eyes in the glinting surface.

'Isabella!' Cassie wanted to grab her, shake her. She stood up, clenching her fists. 'Don't you care about what's happening around here?'

'Of course!' Isabella shouted, turning on her heel. 'Of course I do. I'm so sorry about Yusuf, but I . . . I can't do anything. What do you expect me to do?'

'If you'd seen him you wouldn't be so cavalier,' said Cassie bitterly. 'He washed up on the beach. Richard and I found him. And . . .' She hesitated, staring at Isabella, desperate for any sign of the old friend who would have been bursting with concern for Cassie at this point. But Isabella was like stone, impenetrable. 'And he was hardly recognisable. He looked like . . . he looked like Keiko. Just like she did, after that Knife went into her. Dried up. Mummified.'

'He looked like *Jake's sister*, you mean. After Jess was *drained of all her life-force*.' Isabella's tone had turned very cold.

'Yes! Like Jess, then! Isabella, why are you being like this?'

'I could ask you the same question.' The Argentinian girl stood up abruptly and faced her. 'What are you implying, Cassie? Jake has the Knife, you know that as much as I do. But you seriously think he's running round Istanbul murdering students? Oh, you know him *really* well, don't you!'

'That's not fair—'

'Why not?' snapped Isabella, eyes flashing. 'It's fairer than what you're saying! Mikhail's dead? Yusuf's dead, he looks like that knife killed him? Oh, and Jake just *happens* to be in Istanbul, which you only know because Sir Alric spies on him! My God, you've changed.'

Cassie gaped at her, unable to speak, but Isabella only glared, arms folded. At last she stuttered, 'I'm sorry, Isabella, it's just that I'm worried about Ranjit. He's the only one still missing . . .'

'Oh, I *see*. And Jake thinks Ranjit killed his sister, so you're accusing Jake, who used to be your *friend*, Cassie Bell, of killing *him*! How could you?'

That did it. Her own rage raced back. 'How *could* I? Jake would do anything to get back at Ranjit! Even though he hasn't got a *shred* of proof that Ranjit did anything to Jess! He's so bloody prejudiced against anyone who's Few, he'd—'

'Oh, yes, the precious Few,' sneered Isabella. 'Your new friends. Such good new friends, you can't be bothered with the old ones. Well, you know what,

Cassie? You're welcome to them, and they're welcome to you. It's isn't some spirit that's changed you. You've done it all by yourself!'

'Isabella—'

'Don't even talk to me. I don't want to hear it.' Isabella grabbed her bag and a sweater, and stormed to the door. 'I don't want to be near you right now.'

Cassie couldn't watch her leave. She put her hands over her mouth, blinking back tears of shock and frustration, until the door slammed with an apocalyptic crash. When Isabella's footsteps had faded, she sank back on to the bed and stared in disbelief at her own mirrored image.

Her heart was thundering, and she put a hand to her chest. That reminded her of Estelle, who, right on cue, chimed in.

Cassandra, what have you done? We're already hungry, my dear, we must be careful, we mustn't lose her . . .

'Shut up, Estelle,' Cassie murmured bitterly. She felt rotten. Sheer, bloddy, miserably awful. The last thing she wanted in the world was to fall out with Isabella, and she didn't give a damn right now as to whether Estelle was concerned about keeping her appetite in check.

Even that horrible fight was only the surface, she knew it. Isabella had probably been wanting to spit those words at her for most of the term, and maybe there was some truth in them. There was a lot more to it, though. Cassie knew how much Isabella loved Jake. She knew her friend's ferocious, burning loyalty, and how violently she defended those she loved; it was just that she'd never been on the receiving end before.

But there was more. Isabella was hiding something.

The girl hadn't been surprised about Jake being here. The Isabella Cassie knew would have leaped up, whooping, and demanded they go searching for him that very moment. No, Isabella had known Jake was in Istanbul, and if she knew that, then she'd also been in contact with him. She wouldn't *not*.

And layered over everything was the memory of Yusuf's body, and Cassie's certainty that the Knife was responsible for the state of it. What if . . . what if Ranjit . . . She couldn't bring herself to add that all into the equation. She could only hope. Wait.

But since they'd wrenched it from Keiko's grip, only one person beside herself had had access to that blade.

Jake Johnson.

CHAPTER EIGHTEEN

Cassie woke wishing she had another hangover; anything would be better than feeling the way she did. That brown dove was squatting complacently on the windowsill again, cooing its head off. She flung her bedside book at it, missing by a mile, and it took off with an indignant flapping of wings. In the new silence she slumped back, then heard a muezzin begin to call from some mainland minaret. Then another. Groaning, Cassie pulled her pillow over her head.

She'd heard Isabella leave an hour earlier, but she just wasn't up to facing her roommate, so she'd kept her eyes shut and her breathing regular, and Isabella had left in very unusual silence. Each had known the other was awake, but both of them had kept up the pretence.

It wasn't as if the girl had had an early night; Cassie had heard her creep in very late. She suspected Isabella had known she was still awake then, too, but just like this morning they had both pretended otherwise. Not a word had passed between them since their bitter quarrel.

And this morning there she was, up and out without so much as a good morning. Cassie sat up and ran her hands miserably through her hair. Since when did Isabella choose an early breakfast? This whole situation was unbearable.

No point trying to get back to sleep, not with her head whirling like this. She couldn't really blame muezzin and birds. Cassie headed for the shower, realising why she hated hearing the morning sounds. Even for one morning, she missed Isabella's snoring, her grunts and loud yawns as she woke; she missed her cheerful morning bitching about the godforsaken hour.

As she trudged to her maths class with a heavy heart, Cassie felt more alone than ever. No one seemed to want to speak to her or sit with her; no one even met her eye. Maybe she was getting paranoid, but Herr Stolz's was about the only friendly face in the room, until Richard, Ayeesha and Cormac sloped in; even the other Few ignored her.

To her face, at least. Behind her back they were taking plenty of notice.

She couldn't miss the whispers, the looks, the muttered

asides. No sniggers: at least she wasn't being laughed at. And, though she strained her ears to check, so far no more brutal discoveries seemed to have been made.

Herr Stolz must have been well aware of the events of last night, and Cassie's part in them, because he was kindness itself, giving her far too much attention, too many encouraging smiles, and more than her fair share of quiz questions. It did help, if only a little. She loved maths: its certainty, its simplicity, its capacity to take your mind off finding a greasy mummified corpse on your doorstep. Equations, she thought. God love 'em. She was aware that Richard was watching her surreptitiously, but she chose not to return his look. Algebra was a lot more soothing.

Soothing?

So where did she get the notion that Richard was remotely unnerving? Perhaps it was just the memory of their last encounter together, how it ended . . .

By the time the bell rang, she was involved enough to be sorry the class was over. She could have used double maths today. She was pleased though, that she was finally able to catch Torvald before he left the classroom. She tapped his shoulder and he turned, his face serious as though he could guess what she wanted to ask.

'Listen, I'm . . . I'm getting pretty worried about Ranjit.

Do you know anything, has he had to go away or something?'

Torvald watched her warily. 'I was going to ask you the same thing.'

Cassie blinked. 'How would I know?'

'Well. I thought it might be Few stuff at first. You know? I don't always hear what's happening. I thought there might be . . . an emergency.'

'Me too. I thought maybe with his family.' Cassie bit her lip. 'He hadn't mentioned anything?'

'No. He's just disappeared.' Torvald inhaled deeply. 'Look, I'll let you know as soon as I hear anything.' Cassie nodded, knowing that Torvald's expression was just as worried and doubtful as her own.

Cassie sighed as she left the classroom. She was dreading walking the gauntlet of gossiping Few in the corridor – and with good reason, it seemed.

'Dear heaven, if it isn't the Curse of Cassandra. Get out while you can, everyone.'

Sara seemed determined to get in digs at every turn for what had happened at Carnegie Hall, thought Cassie as she tried to push past the little gang. Funny that Sara was too scared to face her alone – she always had to have a gang around, unsurprisingly – but was she ever going to get tired of baiting her?

Nope . . .

'First Mikhail, now Yusuf. I wonder when she'll consider her revenge complete? Perhaps she's saving the best for last.'

Cassie came to a halt. Clutching her books hard, she turned and stared at Sara. 'What are you talking about?'

Sara didn't answer her directly. She examined her nails with a bored expression, but her comrades glowered at Cassie like a herd of malevolent cows.

'You'd think she'd be grateful, sad little care-home girl. We brought her into the Few, gave her power beyond her wildest imaginings. Or – let's face it – ours.'

'Funny, as I recall, the cowards who so generously initiated me into the Few seemed pretty keen to hide their identities behind some fetching *hoods*,' Cassie hissed.

'Well, yes. But that's why you've done this, isn't it?'

'Yusuf and Mikhail were . . . they were at the Arc de Triomphe?' Cassie found she was shaking.

'Oh don't play the innocent, it *so* doesn't suit you.' Sara smirked. 'I'd better watch my own step, hadn't I, seeing as I was there, too. And, yes, Yusuf and Mikhail, of course, but it's too late for those poor sods.'

Blood had drained from Cassie's face. 'I didn't know that! Any of it!'

'Of course you didn't. Dear.'

'How am I supposed to have known which of you were there? That was the whole point, wasn't it? What do you think, I had X-ray vision or something?' she spat. People had begun to back away from the arguing pair, exchanging worried glances, but Cassie barely noticed.

'Heaven knows how *you* might have discovered these things,' Sara retorted. 'You seem to have all sorts of odd abilities, and I certainly know all about your temper, you little chavski – or should I say, what happens when you lose it. Oh, by the way! We're all wondering when Ranjit's bloated corpse is going to float ashore. Bet *he's* regretting slumming it in the romance department—'

'BITCH!' shouted Cassie. She forgot her composure, forgot even her power, simply dropping her books to lunge for Sara with her bare hands. But as Sara skipped swiftly back, someone shouldered between them, catching Cassie in his arms.

'Ignore her,' whispered Richard fiercely in her ear. 'It's what she wants.'

Panting for breath, Cassie felt her fingertips biting into his biceps with her rage, but he didn't flinch. He turned on Sara like a rattlesnake.

'Back off, you overrated tart,' he snarled.

Some of the others gasped, shocked, but Sara had already recovered her chilly dignity. She soothed them with a regally waved hand, and then jerked a thumb in Richard's direction.

'Little worm,' she drawled. 'He's turning so fast, he'll soon be spinning in his grave if he's not careful.'

Richard took his own advice, ignoring Sara and dragging Cassie away. She was glad of his support for her trembling legs, but less glad that he was stopping her tearing out Sara's throat with her teeth.

'Come on,' he was murmuring. 'You can't rise to it. You mustn't. Why don't we get back to your room and rip up some pillows instead, eh, beautiful?'

She couldn't help her shaky laugh, but it was perilously close to tears. 'I didn't lay a finger on Yusuf or Mikhail, I swear.'

'Of course you didn't. Don't be ridiculous. And don't let her get to you.'

The walk was a blur of fury and misery. If she'd only remembered to use her power, if she hadn't just resorted to the old Cranlake Crescent Cassie, oh, she could have got the better of Sara . . .

Or maybe, just maybe, she might have killed her. Cassie gave a violent shudder.

Coming back to herself, recognising the rugs and sconces and carvings of her own corridor, she shook Richard off gently. Breathing deeply, she turned to face him.

'Richard.' She reached for both his hands and clasped them tightly between hers. 'How do you stand it? *Tell me.*'

'Stand what?' The old familiar shutters were coming down all of a sudden, and the beginnings of a false grin twitched his mouth.

'Stop that, Richard. Stop joking about it! You know what I mean: they treat you like a pet! I mean – sometimes they indulge you, and sometimes it pleases their majesties to give you a bloody good *kicking*.' Hearing the venom in her voice, she gulped hard, struggling to control herself. Struggling not to see the world in scarlet . . .

Richard's grin subsided and he studied her, very thoughtfully. 'Well, does that bother you? How they treat me?'

'Yes! It bloody does!'

The corners of his lips once again began to turn up, but this time it was genuine. 'Good to know you care,' he said, almost to himself.

The taut knot of rage dissolved on the spot, leaving her so weak she almost stumbled. Cassie sighed raggedly as he caught her arm.

'Anyway, I think you know the answer to your own question, since we can't all host a spirit as powerful as Estelle Azzedine's.' He shrugged. 'As for my poor little blighter . . . I don't know how it's lasted this long, to be honest. I don't know who hosted it before me, but I reckon it's always played both sides against the middle. Always ducking out by the skin of its teeth, I imagine, while the rest of the Few tear each other to sexily attractive shreds.' Now it was his turn to exhale.

'Sod that,' she countered. 'There's at least one of us you can't play.'

He smiled, and nodded. 'Go on home.' He placed his hand on the small of her back and edged her gently in the direction of her door. 'You need some rest.'

'Thanks.' She turned the handle, grinning weakly back at him. 'I mean it, Richard. Thanks.' But as she took a step inside, Cassie froze.

'Oh my God . . .' she breathed.

Richard was back at her side in an instant, staring around the room along with her.

All trace of Isabella had disappeared from the room. Her photos, her books, her iPod – everything was gone from her nightstand, and her haphazard pile of make-up had been cleared from the dressing table. When Cassie ran to the wardrobe and flung it open, it was empty of dresses and coats, jumpers and shoes – and so was the chest of drawers. Isabella's schoolwork and her laptop had disappeared. Cassie stood in the middle of their

189

room, half expecting the whole world to disintegrate around her.

Richard was at Isabella's made-up bed, lifting a smooth white envelope. 'She left a note,' he said. 'I suppose that's something.'

Cassie took it from him, ripping it open with her thumb. It took only a moment to scan her best friend's untidy handwriting. She sat down heavily on Isabella's bed, and when Richard sat down next to her and put an arm round her shoulder, she didn't shrug him off.

Cassie dropped the letter, and it floated to the floor. 'She's moved in with Alice. Just for a while, she says. To give her time to think.' She made a twisted face to stop herself bursting into tears. 'It's not for ever, apparently. It's just *for now*.'

'Blimey.' Richard squeezed her. 'It's been pretty crap between you two, hasn't it? But this is a bit of a shock.'

'You could say that.' Cassie rubbed her face with her sleeve.

'Cassie. What happened between the two of you? Was it Jake?'

She nodded. 'My fault. We kept the feeding from him. When he found out, he went into a rage, stormed off. I haven't seen him since. Obviously it's all been really hard for Isabella to deal with.'

They sat together in silence as it sank in. At last Richard sighed, and rubbed the fingers of his free hand against his temple.

'*You* haven't seen him since?'

'What?'

'You said *you* haven't seen him, Cassie. I heard your emphasis.'

'Yeah.' Her voice sounded very small. 'That's the trouble. Jake's in Istanbul.'

Richard's whole body froze; she could feel his muscles practically go into spasm. 'He's *what*? What would he be doing . . . ?'

'He's in Istanbul. I haven't seen him, but Darke knows it for sure. And I think—'

'Whoa.' Richard was still as tense as a drum. 'You think Isabella's seeing him?'

'I'm pretty sure. And she's keeping it quiet. And I don't know why she'd do that unless . . .'

'Oh, God almighty.' Richard released her, put his head in his hands and ran his hands quickly through his hair. 'Jessica, Ranjit, the Few, revenge . . . it's OK, Cassie, I'm getting there. I'm not as stupid as I make out.'

'Tell me, though.' Cassie stared at her hands, twisting them together. 'Was Sara telling me the truth back there? About who was at my initiation?'

'Yes. Yes, that was true.'

'So if Jake has somehow found that out too . . .' Cassie put her hand over her mouth for a moment, feeling sick. 'He could be trying to set me up?'

'Oh, come on. I can't believe he'd be involved with the deaths.'

'I don't want to believe it myself, but then why's he lying bloody low?' She gave him a bleak look.

'And you reckon Isabella's helping him?'

'I can't imagine she wouldn't,' said Cassie miserably. 'She loves him.'

'And we're all suckers for love.' Richard was silent for a moment. 'What a mess.'

Cassie took another look around her room – her now-single room – and felt hot tears slide down her face. 'What am I going to do?'

'She'll come around. She's all right, our bella Isabella. She wouldn't know a grudge if it came up and slapped her arse.'

She couldn't even laugh. 'It's not that. I mean, not *just* that.'

'Oh.' Alarmed, Richard took her chin gently in his fingers and turned her to face him. 'When did you last feed?'

'A while ago,' she confessed miserably. 'The night of the

192

island party. And not much even then.'

'OK.' He patted her cheek gently, leaned in to kiss it, then got swiftly to his feet. 'I can't help with a lot of things, Cassie, but this is one thing I *can* sort out. And you don't have to be grateful for more than, oh, two or three centuries, really, doll. Yes, I can definitely give you some concrete, tasty help with this one . . .'

CHAPTER NINETEEN

Nervously Cassie tapped once, lightly, on the door before her, withdrawing her fist swiftly to chew on her fingernails. She eyed the polished plaque with trepidation.

RICHARD HALTON-JONES
PEREGRINE HUTTON

The door eased silently open, so that she saw first his fingers, then, as his face appeared, a solemn wink. Richard raised one finger to his lips and pulled the door wider.

'Shh. He's in the Land of Nod. Well, more or less.'

Beyond Richard's shoulder she had quite a good view of the room. It wasn't dissimilar to hers and Isabella's, but perhaps even more opulent: plenty of gilding, lots of baroque, lashings of Ottoman chic. And if anything it was tidier than the room she'd just left, except for the silk scarf hanging from the chandelier. She wondered if Richard had been swinging on it. Wouldn't put it past him.

He reached for her hand, but she stepped back abruptly, resisting. 'Richard, I don't know if this is such a good idea . . .'

He tutted. 'You haven't really got a choice, Cassie. You're looking rather pale already, you know.'

'But—'

'No ifs, no buts. He's not that bad.'

Cassie wrinkled her nose. She hadn't even been thinking about . . . flavour . . . as being part of her trepidation. 'Uh, are you sure?'

'Well, he wouldn't be to everyone's taste, but I have to say, I quite like him.' Richard wiggled his eyebrows. 'Come on.'

Reluctantly Cassie stepped all the way into the room, getting an instant whiff of male cologne.

'His, not mine,' whispered Richard, sniffing the air. 'It has a bloody footballer on the box, for God's sake. Give me Antaeus any day. Anyway, beautiful, enough small talk. Bon appetit.'

He gestured towards Perry, who was lounging in an armchair, arms hanging over the sides, one leg crossed nonchalantly over the other. Cassie wouldn't have thought there was anything particularly wrong, were it not for the boy's aimless smile and unfocused eyes.

'Richard, has he been . . . drinking?' She narrowed her eyes.

'Course he has. You don't think he's in on this, do you? He's not the type to be understanding, not like your Isa—' Richard caught himself, and gave her an apologetic grimace. 'Damn. Sorry.'

'I don't know – I'm not used to feeding from people who don't know what's going on. That Few drink, I don't know . . . and Sir Alric would—'

'To hell with *him*.' Richard walked across to his roommate and patted his cheek gently. 'Hey, Peregrine? Visitors.'

'Mm?' Perry tried to focus on Cassie, who smiled at him nervously. 'What's she doing here?'

Richard smiled. 'None of your business.'

'Oh . . . very well . . .' Perry's head lolled back and he grinned up at Richard, who took his hands and brought him to his feet.

'Good God, Peregrine,' Richard said, with a brief look at Cassie. 'Were you at the Chablis again while my back was turned?'

' 'S delicious,' said Perry. 'Hello, Cassandra.' He gave her a leering wink that didn't quite come off.

'Sit on the bed, you dreadful old lush.' Richard nudged him down on to it. 'Come on, sit straight.'

Perry tilted woozily, righted himself and giggled. Shutting one eye, he watched Cassie suspiciously as she sat beside him. Richard took her hands firmly and clasped them round Perry's wrists.

'Whoah there, angel,' Perry objected, eyeing Cassie's hands. 'No offence, you being Few and all, but you're not my type.'

Anxiously Cassie glanced at Richard, but he shook his head. 'Ignore him. He won't remember a thing, will you, Peregrine? Right, Cassie, off you go.'

'Richard, I'm not sure. I mean, I'm not used to him. What if I go too far?'

'Trust me, you won't, beautiful. I need to feed as well, so I want half myself. Honestly, don't worry, I'll stop you.'

Oh for heaven's sake, Cassandra. He'll do!

Estelle was right: she was hungry. They both were. Taking a deep breath, closing her eyes to focus, Cassie began to feed.

He was different from Isabella, that was for sure. As his life-force throbbed out of his veins and poured into her, she felt the usual heady fizz of youth. But it wasn't the same. She felt a distinctive maleness. It surged through her, almost knocking her backwards, but as she opened her reddening eyes and righted herself, she felt the essence of him filling her. He was all arrogance, confidence, a petulant sense of entitlement; and for a moment so was Cassie. Pride expanded her ribcage. She was *elite*. Always had been, always would be.

And then Richard was prising her hands from Perry's wrists, gently but firmly. As the link broke she stumbled back, satisfied. The pulse in her chest faded with the red light of her eyes.

Not at all like Isabella. Not nearly as good. But he certainly plugged the gap for the time being.

'My turn.' Richard took her place, clasped his thumbs over Perry's wrists and began to feed.

She didn't leave it too long, or at least she didn't think she had. Cassie assumed Richard's weaker spirit had nothing like the appetite and the needs of Estelle. When Cassie judged he'd taken about half a feeding, she put a hand on his shoulder, and he broke off without effort, pausing for his eyes to return to normal. He was breathing a little faster as he stood up, but then gave a short intake of breath.

'Damn,' he said.

'What is it?'

Richard nodded at Perry. The boy's eyes were half open, but they were glazed and blurry. Slowly, like a toppling tree, he fell backwards, sprawled across the bed, a feeble sigh escaping his lips.

Richard leaned over him, pressing his ear to his chest.

'Tell me he's alive,' begged Cassie faintly.

'Course he is.' Richard stood up, sounding relieved. 'I think we might have overdone that a bit. But he'll be fine.'

Perry's eyes drifted shut and he fell asleep with an idiotic smile still on his face. Richard puffed out a relieved breath.

'OK. If you're sure.' Cassie shook herself, still feeling a little strange with Perry's essence inside her, but it was subsiding now, swallowed up by her own life and Estelle's. 'Listen, thanks, Richard. I do appreciate this, really. You're very generous, but I really don't think I can do it all the time.'

'You'll have to. Till Isabella snaps out of it.'

'I know. But I hate having to drug someone – even *him* – and it's not exactly safe, is it? We've got no idea how far to go when there's two of us.'

'I'm sure we'll get the hang of it.'

She shook her head firmly. 'I'll find an alternative. I don't want to end up killing somebody.' Somebody *else*, she added mentally. 'Anyway, half a feeding isn't really enough, is it?'

'Not for you, that's for sure. I could just about manage,

but . . . well.' Richard shrugged. 'It's a stopgap.'

'Thanks again, Richard.'

'Any time,' he said, his eyes locking on hers. 'And listen, beautiful, I mean that. Anything I can do to help.'

It seemed perfectly natural to lean into him. His spirit might not be the strongest, but as pure boy he was all protective chivalry, and she found she needed that. Almost instinctively, she wrapped her arms around him, and he returned the hug, squeezing her teasingly, then leaving his arms to relax around her comfortingly. Pulling back a little and turning her face up to his, her arms still wrapped around his muscular torso, Cassie studied Richard's face closely. It was getting so familiar. She found she liked it. A lot. Even more when it was leaning closer to hers, lips slightly parted, eyes a little puzzled . . .

Wait, no. This was crazy, wasn't it?

And yet it felt so natural, the way they leaned in towards each other. He was a friend, she thought. A *good* friend, as it turned out. And she really needed a friend right now.

So, kiss him, or not kiss him? A no-brainer. Kiss him . . .

'Richaaaard?'

He blinked, bit his lip. When he spoke, Richard's voice was husky. 'Damn. It wasn't you that said that, was it?'

She gave him a wry smile, drew back, and shook her head.

As they both turned back towards the bed, Perry was half sitting up, rubbing his temples and frowning blearily at the pair of them. 'Richard? What in God's name is she doing here?'

'You're repeating yourself, old boy,' murmured Richard, too low for him to hear, but Cassie had to muffle a giggle.

'My cue to leave,' she whispered.

'Mm, I suppose so. I'll look after the, er . . . the night-time snacks.' He grinned, but there was a definite expression of regret on his face. 'See you soon?'

She nodded, and smiled, her heart still thudding. 'Yeah. See you soon.'

Closing the door behind her and sighing as she faced the corridor and the walk back, Cassie felt heartsick at the prospect of a lonely night in her own empty room. And shocked to her core at how much she had wanted to stay in that one.

CHAPTER TWENTY

They couldn't go on like this. Cassie knew it as soon as she opened her eyes next morning and saw Isabella's neatly made and empty bed. Not just because of the dangerous business with Perry – God, she thought with a sickening jolt, how could they have done something so risky? – but because she couldn't bear not having Isabella around. Whatever was wrong, it had to be fixable. She'd never had a friend like Isabella and she was damned if she was going to lose her. And what was more, with each passing day, the threat of something bad having happened to Ranjit seemed to grow more and more likely. If there was some connection with Jake, or something Isabella knew that might help, Cassie was determined to find out.

She didn't want to go to Alice's room; she did not want to run into Alice, or worse, the two of them together. But, despite her ridiculously svelte figure, Isabella always ate a huge breakfast; she was bound to be later leaving the dining room than Alice. Cassie could ambush her there.

Hovering in the great domed atrium near the dining room corridor, listening to the sounds of breakfast without feeling any compulsion to eat it herself, Cassie crossed her fingers. Apart from anything else, she was getting downright jealous of the amount of time Isabella and Alice were spending together. She dreaded to think how they might bitch about the disadvantages of room-sharing with Few – and what Isabella might let slip . . .

However, there was no sign of Alice yet. Killing time by wandering among the familiar statues, Cassie was so certain Alice would come out first, she almost missed Isabella. If she hadn't heard the click of Jimmy Choos—

Hurrying from the dining room, Isabella didn't even see her; she was too intently focused on her phone, which was pressed to her ear. But some instinct stopped Cassie from dashing out to intercept her. In the shadow of Odysseus and Circe, she went quite still, pressed against the cold marble of the witch's robe. There was a bright excited light in her roommate's eyes.

Isabella was talking animatedly, but Cassie was well used to the gabbling speed of her voice. Together with her Few senses, heightened after last night's feeding, that meant she could catch almost every word. Which wasn't doing anything for her peace of mind.

'Fifteen minutes . . . no, twenty . . . will that do? Of course I'll be there . . .' Her voice lowered, but it remained urgent. 'Yes, of course I'll be careful. Don't worry. Nobody will see me . . . OK? Good!'

She wasn't even going back upstairs. Her bag was over her shoulder and she was already out of the door and running down the Academy steps.

Cassie knew she had only a moment to decide. Saturday morning. The bigger ferry boat would be in use, and it would be busy with students going into the city. She could lose herself in the crowd. Besides, if Isabella did see her, would it matter? She was going into town alone. To sightsee. Browse in the Grand Bazaar. Perfectly natural. No worries . . .

Her mind made up, Cassie walked swiftly out of the Academy, pretending not to hear Ayeesha calling after her. She'd been right: there was already a large gaggle of students gathered on the small pier, laughing with the freedom of the weekend. She could see Isabella's glossy chestnut hair blowing in the breeze, up towards the prow.

Cassie slipped into the back of the crowd, making sure she was last to board. Not having a bag may have looked a bit suspect, but at least she had her battered wallet in her jeans pocket, with enough lira for emergencies. Ignoring everyone around her, but shouldering deftly through a gang of third years who were tall and numerous enough to hide her, she leaned over the stern and watched the boat's wake churn the Bosphorus.

What was she doing? She knew very well how she'd feel if someone spied on her. If Isabella found out, she'd be incandescent, and it would probably put paid to their relationship altogether – which, considering Cassie had come downstairs this morning determined to repair things between them, was a little ironic.

She couldn't help it. She was as sure as she could be that Isabella had been talking to Jake, and not only that: she'd just arranged to meet him. That, she told herself firmly, was proof that Isabella, too, had sabotaged their relationship. She'd been in contact with Jake. She'd hidden that from Cassie. Isabella, too, was being devious. But perhaps this was her chance – to let Isabella lead her to Jake, and get to the bottom of what was going on.

Oh hell. Either way, the potential for proof of Isabella's betrayal didn't make her feel any better. By the time the boat docked at the mainland, Cassie's heart was thudding with nerves and guilt and the fear of discovery. She was so careful to let everyone leave the boat before her, to stay well back from Isabella, she almost lost her. Which was a stupid risk, and quite unnecessary. When Cassie did spot her again, moving swiftly through the crowds, Isabella seemed oblivious to everything but her mission.

The streets were thronged. Cassie almost wished she could loiter and enjoy the atmosphere. The air was hot and smelled of musty ancient buildings, of men's cologne, of strong tobacco smoke and spices and roasting nuts. Elegant shops jostled for space with junk emporiums and street vendors.

It struck Cassie that she was wasting practically her entire school career in intrigue and deception. Hell, it would have been fun to experience all this *alongside* Isabella, laughing and talking and ogling ancient monuments, haggling for bargains and triumphing over successes. That's how it should have been. Normal school life would have been good. It would have been more than enough for a care-home-raised scholarship girl.

Instead, she was tailing her erstwhile best friend through the streets and alleys of Sultanahmet, and it was no mean task. Without her Few senses she'd have lost her long ago, but despite all the scents and sounds of the city, Cassie could still smell Isabella's distinctive perfume – and even the scent of her skin – tracking her without difficulty even when she lost sight of her.

Isabella didn't stop even for the glossiest of shops, the

most enchanting of silks or jewels or carpets. It was so unlike her, Cassie was more than ever convinced she was heading for a rendezvous with Jake. The Grand Bazaar? The Argentinian girl seemed to be heading that way, through Beyazit, and for all her remarks about a tourist trap, it would be the ideal place for a secret meeting.

Yes. Cassie dodged round jewellery stalls and kofte vendors in time to see Isabella disappear into one of the southern entrances. She darted after her, no longer afraid of being seen. She was confident now that she could stay close to her quarry till she reached her rendezvous.

It was an unpleasant surprise, then, when Isabella simply walked briskly through the covered streets, ignoring all the shops, and back out of the western entrance.

When Isabella stopped and pulled out her phone, Cassie swore to herself and pulled back, turning swiftly to a vendor selling roasted sweetcorn. A heartbeat later, Isabella was walking on. Once more Cassie followed, beginning to feel a deep degree of stupid.

Isabella didn't go much farther, though: only as far as the shady trees and canopies of the Book Bazaar. Here she seemed to hesitate, then found her bearings again and hurried down a paved lane crammed with bookstalls. After a while, she stopped quite deliberately, and spoke to a stallholder.

Cassie ducked into another little shop, half hiding behind a rack of maps and pamphlets. What was going on? There was no sign of Jake, but Isabella was handing the bookseller an envelope, and he was opening it to flick through what was inside.

Notes. Money. Cassie was sure of it.

The bookseller reached down below his counter, drawing something out. As he handed it to Isabella, Cassie craned dangerously far out from her hiding place, desperate to see it. But it was too small, and too far away. As Isabella smiled and turned abruptly, Cassie ducked back behind the rack, not breathing, focusing intently on an antique map of Turkey.

Her former roommate strode back determinedly the way she had come, passing quite close to Cassie but – thank heavens – failing to glance to her right. Cassie felt the thrashing of her heart begin to subside, and she took a few deep breaths. She was as sure as she could be that Isabella's rendezvous was over, that that had been it.

What had been it? Slowly Cassie followed Isabella back through the Grand Bazaar, at a greater distance this time. The girl was in less of a hurry now, browsing idly for scarves and *kilims* and brooches, stopping to buy herself a small bag of pistachios, then bartering for a slender gold bracelet. But there was little doubt she was heading back to the pier and the boat, and when she turned down the lane to the waterside, Cassie at last gave up the chase.

There didn't seem much point in risking getting caught on the same boat as Isabella this time. She would hang back and wait for the next one: no way was she pushing her luck any further. Lingering in the narrow lane, back against the old stone, she wondered what on earth to do next. She had a good bit of time to kill till the Academy ferry returned.

What had been the point? She'd thought she was on to something, thought she would solve at least one of the wretched mysteries that were dogging her, but she'd wasted her time, wasted half the energy she'd drained out of Perry. She'd lost her chance to make it up with Isabella; instead she'd spied on her like a thief. And she'd also failed to find Jake, and so was no closer to finding out where Ranjit was. Or what had happened to him. Adrenalin seeped out of her like water out of a sponge. She was empty, drained and miserable.

Maybe that was why, very suddenly, she knew the tables had turned on her.

Someone's watching us!

Yes.

Cassie went absolutely still. Estelle was right. She'd felt that strong sense before, that knowledge that she was being watched. Before, when they'd been in Cukurcuma! Taking a moment to psyche herself up, she drew a deep breath, then spun on her heel.

A small movement; barely enough to be seen, but someone had ducked behind that high building at the end of the alleyway. Cassie narrowed her eyes, then sprinted back, flinging herself round the corner.

Nothing. No one.

She stopped, breathing hard, uncertain. Had there been anyone, or was it nothing but her overactive imagination again?

Oh, stop lying to yourself, dearest! You know when you're being watched. You know as well as I do.

'Estelle,' she murmured. 'Estelle, was it him? Was it Ranjit?'

For seconds Estelle was silent, as if Cassie had taken her by surprise.

Dear oh dear, Cassandra. You mustn't maintain this state of denial. Of course it wasn't him!

Cassie was aware of the stares she was attracting – standing here talking to herself like a madwoman – but she was annoyed enough to snap at Estelle. 'How would you know?' she hissed.

We had a history, his spirit and I, long before you joined our little soirée . . .

'Well, I've felt this before. I've been followed, by *Ranjit*, and I know what his eyes . . . h-his eyes watching me feels like!' She took several deep breaths, desperate tears stinging her eyes. Yet the spirit was unrelenting.

Ha! You think I don't? You're wrong, my dear. You're believing what you want to believe.

Angrily Cassie shook her off. Was it wishful thinking, to imagine Ranjit was tailing her footsteps, silent for some unfathomable reason but unable to leave her alone? It seemed so absurdly unlikely, after all.

But that *was* how it had felt the last time. It was the same strong tingle of fearful anticipation she'd felt when Ranjit had stalked her through the corridors of a Paris mansion. She'd been so sure, when she turned that corner, she'd see those roiling, gold-glowing, animal eyes. To be so hopeful – and then so mistaken – was a bitter blow to her heart. And it came on top of the horrible realisation that she was so very lonely, that she missed Isabella like crazy.

OK, she had to calm down. So she was either getting paranoid and developing a persecution complex, or someone sinister really was following her. Neither option boded well for her social life – or her life in general. Whichever it was, she'd better keep her strength up . . .

A kofte vendor on the pavement beside her was eyeing

her with visible nerves. Cassie shook herself, and managed a strained smile. She was unexpectedly hungry: that unassuageable hunger that meant she hadn't fed enough, or had used up too much energy. Kofte would be the most temporary of stopgaps, but she bought one anyway, stuffed with roasted peppers between chunks of oily bread. She bit into it with such ferocity that the stallholder flinched and pretended to look the other way.

CHAPTER TWENTY-ONE

It wasn't as if Latin was her favourite or her best subject. It had waited all these centuries; it could manage another ninety minutes without her. Cassie wasn't willing to wait another single one, let alone an interminable *double* period of bloody Virgil. Yusuf and Mikhail were dead, and Ranjit might be next. He might already— No! She refused even to contemplate the possibility. But with still no word from him, Cassie was now adamant that it was time to take the initiative.

There was only one place to start looking. Cassie went straight to Ranjit's room, half hoping that it would be empty and that she'd have peace to prowl, but it wasn't to be. When the door began to open to her knock, her breath caught in her throat and her heart leaped – irrational as it was, she couldn't help hoping against hope that she'd see Ranjit's face – but it was Torvald again.

'Cassie.' He eyed her, puzzled, but his overriding expression was one of anxiety.

'Sorry to disturb you—' she began, her words tumbling out.

Torvald held up his hand to stop her. 'Don't worry about it. Still nothing, I'm afraid. I don't suppose you've . . . ?'

Cassie shook her head, her brow furrowed. Torvald stepped back, gesturing. 'Look, why don't you come in? No point standing out here.'

She nodded. As he followed her in and shut the door, Torvald said, 'He hasn't been around for ages.'

'I don't get it. I mean, he'd tell you if he had to go away, wouldn't he?'

'Usually.' He shrugged.

Cassie swallowed. 'Well . . . I mean, of course he's always kind of been a law unto himself, right? Maybe we're worrying too much . . .'

'Yes, but he's never been away for so long,' pointed out Torvald. 'And he always told me when he'd be back.'

I'll bet he did, thought Cassie dryly. Hungry after an absence, poor lad.

'Have you talked to Sir Alric?'

'I've tried. Didn't get any joy out of him. He's aware of the situation, that's all he would say.'

Cassie turned a slow circle, studying the boys' room, opulent as ever. They even had a flat-screen TV. Torvald certainly got good perks for feeding Ranjit. She wondered if he knew.

Maybe her nosiness was a bit blatant, because he said rather pointedly, 'There might be a clue here that I'm missing. Do you want to check a few things?'

She raised an eyebrow. 'Have you looked through his stuff?'

'Course I have. Nothing's missing, not his passport, no clothes, not even his wallet. He's just – kind of – evaporated.'

'His emails? Anything like that?' Cassie was wandering round the room now, touching things. Something was making her deeply uneasy. It was as if she could feel his presence . . . and something else too, fainter though. Something familiar, or *someone* she knew? That something or someone had been here and she could feel its former presence like a ghost. A ghost she could smell and touch. What it reminded her of most was . . .

The Knife.

That was it. She had a connection to that strange Few artefact, with its bizarre inward life. When it was close, it spoke to her like a voice. Well, this was the same sort of feeling. It had been in here at some point, she was almost certain of it.

And it wouldn't have got there all by itself. Could Jake have—?

'What are you thinking?' Torvald's voice broke into her thoughts.

'Nothing.' *Nothing you'd want to know, anyway.* Cassie turned to face him. 'Where's Ranjit's laptop?'

'There.' Torvald pulled out a drawer and retrieved it, setting it reverently on the desktop. 'I don't know his password, obviously. Same with the voicemails on the room's phone system. I can't access them.'

'Let me try.' She booted up the laptop, hesitated with her fingers on the keys.

ranjitsingh

Incorrect password

ranjit1

Incorrect password

darkeacademy

Too obvious, anyway. She tapped her fingernails on the edge of the laptop.

No, it couldn't be.

Maybe?

cassandra

Welcome Ranjit

Behind her, Torvald coughed. Cassie stepped back, beating back a rush of conflicting emotions, then bent down to the keyboard again.

There was nothing sinister that she could see: nothing, but the fact that no emails had been downloaded in ages. With a horrible sense of dread, Cassie watched the list of unread emails grow like a black spell, creeping down the screen. Two from his mother. One from his academic counsellor. Amazon, iTunes, play.com, the usual suspects. Fifteen, twenty . . . She didn't know he subscribed to popbitch.com, she thought with a small reluctant smile. More emails piled in: another from his mother, now one from his father. His brothers, an email from each.

She pushed back the chair as the list finally stopped. 'Nothing,' she said, though she had a feeling it was anything but. 'I'll try his voicemail.'

It was the same story. Luckily, it was the same password: guilt clenched her stomach. Had he really pined for her as much as Torvald claimed? Unwilling to believe she had found nothing, she sat back down at the laptop and opened a list of his documents in a separate window.

'So what do you think?' Torvald sounded impatient.

'Hang on.' Increasingly frustrated and desperate, she scrolled down the document list. There were so many; should she open every single one? Even if it all looked like innocent homework, there could be useful information disguised behind an inane document name . . .

Something caught her eye. She scrolled back up to it.

Found Items

Not so mysterious, as names went. But it was password protected.

She tried again.

cassandra

No . . .

She chewed on a nail. Well, it was worth a try. She typed in her birth date.

Bingo!

Torvald was leaning over her shoulder, tense with interest, as the PDF of a scanned document loaded. Some kind of manuscript, pages and pages of it. 'What is that? It looks ancient,' he said, his voice tight, curious.

Cassie took a breath. 'Yeah it does, doesn't it? Could be a fake, of course. Something he found on the net . . .'

She was talking nonsense, and she knew it. This was an old document and she knew immediately it was something important. The faded writing was antiquated, but she could just about make it out – and not just that: there were symbols, designs, ancient script similar to images she'd seen before. And one image in particular that she'd seen everywhere from New York Public Library to the Arc de Triomphe to the broken version on her own shoulder blade . . .

She knew one thing: she did not want Torvald peering over her shoulder while she deciphered the document. Swiftly she clicked the print button and closed the window.

'But what was it?' He stepped back, disappointed and a little annoyed.

'I . . . I dunno, really. It might be something or nothing. I'll take a copy and check it out, OK? I, ah . . . have a class now,' she lied.

He scowled. 'All right. I get the message: this is Few stuff, right?' He stopped for a moment, relenting. 'Look. You promise me you'll let me know if you find anything?' He hesitated. 'I miss him too, you know.'

'Course I will.' Forcing what she hoped was an unconcerned smile, she closed the document and rolled up the printout, keeping it well away from his curious gaze. 'As soon as I know anything. But let's not get our hopes up yet, eh?'

She was afraid he was going to delay her further, but he didn't. Once outside Ranjit's room, with the door shut firmly behind her, she ran for her own. It was time to try and figure out what the hell was going on.

CHAPTER TWENTY-TWO

As Cassie got back and closed the door behind her, she took a deep breath and pulled out her desk chair. Placing the printout pages on the smooth wooden desktop, she sat down and shuffled quickly through them, desperate for some clues. The pages were blurred in some places, indecipherable in parts, but she was getting the gist of them just fine. Sitting in the too-quiet room, Cassie could hear the blood rushing in her ears as she ran her forefinger across the heading of the topmost page.

Powers and Nature of the Eldest Few

The Eldest Few. Just the name made her shiver with a sensation that was all Few instinct. It seemed that the very first Few was, according to this document, the most evil of creatures, and as those who succeeded him grew in number, his power had got out of control.

He was apparently the one who created the Knife. With the tip of her finger Cassie traced the picture on the page: the blade, the elaborate handle, the mythical creatures that writhed around it. She involuntarily grimaced, remembering the real thing. Many seemed to hate or fear that blade, but Cassie couldn't bring herself to feel anything but fascination. It was beautiful, and alive, and lethal. Why did she feel such an attraction to it, and what did that say about her?

Something else about the Knife grabbed her attention, and her breath caught in her throat. According to the manuscript, it had a special purpose. The Knife was the only thing able to sever the link between Spirit and Host . . .

*Only this Knife, or Death itself
may break the Bond*

Cassie was stunned. This was the answer she had been looking for at the start of last term, when she'd been so desperate to find a way to get Estelle's spirit out of her for good. She wasn't sure how to feel about the discovery that the means may have been right under her nose that whole time.

No, Cassandra, let us not think back to that dark time. We're together now, we are strong . . .

There was a distinct edge of nerves to Estelle's voice, but Cassie's growing astonishment was drowning her out at the moment.

Because it seemed that the Eldest had created more than just the Knife.

Rubbing her forehead, trying to shift the headache she could not afford right now, Cassie squinted at the text, reading and re-reading the details of the other artefacts – a Pendant and an Urn.

There was something eerily familiar about the pictures of both, as though they'd been formed from the same stuff as the Knife. She touched the scanned engraving of the Pendant. It was carved out of jade, the manuscript told her, but it was like no other piece of jewellery she'd ever seen. As with the Knife, it was carved with twisting, snarling beasts: there they were, the familiar cats and mermaids and caryatids, and the less recognisable creatures she had never been able to name.

*The Pendant may, for a spell of time,
be used to draw the Spirit from its Host.*

Which sounded uncomfortably like what Cassie

thought of as her 'broken' powers – part of Estelle's spirit being locked outside of her, able to invisibly manifest itself in the inexplicable ability she had to control and move and manipulate with her mind alone . . .

And the Urn. As she read the words again, Cassie felt her eyes so wide with amazement that they hurt, and she had to blink hard as she studied the scans of the perfectly inked text.

The Urn may contain and preserve a
Spirit indefinitely.

Why exactly would anyone want to contain and preserve a spirit anywhere but inside a host's body . . . ?

From thence the Spirit's energy may be consumed.
Thus did the Eldest create the greatest Evil,
and thus did the Elders resolve that he, the
Eldest, must be defeated and contained.

Ah. It seemed the Eldest Few had a hunger for more than just your common-or-garden human life-force.

It was all so much to take in. If the Knife was not the only remnant of a lost Few culture, perhaps it *wasn't* the Knife she'd sensed after all in Ranjit's room? It could have been any of the other artefacts. Was it possible that it wasn't the Knife that had killed Yusuf and sucked him as dry as a dead herring? That maybe Jake *wasn't* the culprit?

But if not him, then who?

Cassie shuddered, turning another page. At last, there was some good news, she thought, though she couldn't help noting the irony of seeing this part as a good thing, given all that had happened last term . . .

The Elders had formed a Council (yes, that sounded familiar) that was strong enough to defeat the Eldest Few: he had fled, never to be seen again. The Council, recognising the dreadful power inherent in his creations, had hidden the artefacts. For some reason that she didn't understand, the manuscript said that the artefacts were hidden by *non*-Few, drugged to forget what they'd done and where they'd been (that sounded familiar too, Cassie thought with a frown).

And the records of the artefacts and their hiding places, as deemed by the Council – contained within this manuscript – were to be divided in two. This document that Ranjit had found, it seemed, was only Part One . . .

Cassie sat back, breathing deeply. It sounded crazy, and

only made a vague kind of sense in her mind. Thinking of Jake, she shivered. What had he done with the Knife? Had it fallen into the wrong hands? Was that why Ranjit had been asking about it, was he worried about what it could do? She sighed. So much was still so unclear.

Flipping back through the pages, Cassie smoothed them with her palms, marvelling at the detail in the engravings, even in laser-printed reproduction. Something made her want to touch every one of these beautiful drawings, and to touch their real living counterparts. She could almost feel the warm smoothness of the jade pendant as she ran her fingers across the page. And then, with a heavy heart, she flicked to the final page, where the elegant, barely decipherable script ran out.

Yes, the Knife had been hidden in Angkor Wat, Cambodia; she could make out that much from the description, though the place wasn't named. The hiding place of the Pendant *was* named, though.

Byzantium

Byzantium. Which then became Constantinople. Which then became . . . Istanbul. It had been hidden right there, in that very city. There was no indication of where *exactly* it was hidden; only a sketch of a symbol, different to the familiar Few mark, under which the Pendant apparently lay,

But one thing was clear enough to her: Ranjit had found this manuscript, scanned it, and gone to hunt down the Pendant.

But *why*? And what had happened to him? Maybe the other part of the manuscript explained more?

Cassie knew she couldn't tell Sir Alric about all this. She knew that very clearly. She wasn't going to be the one who got Ranjit into trouble. She'd just have to get him out of it . . .

Somehow.

She needed help, though, and there was only one person now who'd be willing, who she'd – almost – trust. Pulling out her phone, she dialled Richard.

'Richard? Hey. It's Cassie.'

'Like I'd fail to recognise those dulcet tones, beautiful. But you sound tense. Anything I can, uh, help with?'

She could practically hear his grin through the receiver, but she had to ignore it. 'Look, I've found something. Do you think you could come over?'

He was knocking on her door within minutes of her call.

'That's an invitation I can't refuse. What's the mystery, then?'

'Look at this.' She drew him over to the desk, sat him down, and fanned out the pages before him. 'See what you make of it.'

Leaning closer to her, Cassie felt guilt shimmer through her along with the electricity of attraction. Now certainly wasn't the time – not with the situation with Ranjit looking more and more serious with every passing moment.

Richard skimmed the text, quickly turning the pages, occasionally hesitating over an obscured word. It took him perhaps ten minutes to read the lot.

'This certainly makes a lot of things a bit clearer.' Shaking his head, he sat back, touching the papers almost reverently. 'Keiko *did* find that knife in Angkor Wat. I remember it well. It was something she sensed. She was sure something was there, in one of the old temples, but she didn't know what; she was obsessed with tracking it down. And she did. And you know what? She was never quite the same . . .'

Cassie watched him thoughtfully. 'You mean she wasn't always a crazy homicidal bitch?'

Richard laughed. 'A crazy bitch, always. But it was like everything multiplied overnight: the crazy part and the bitch part. And she certainly turned homicidal.'

'Yeah, I know.' Cassie shivered.

'Nobody else was ever allowed to touch it. She was so possessive about the thing. It was like she'd found the One Ring.'

'Hmm,' Cassie mumbled, her brow knit. 'Maybe the artefacts have some strange affect on Few. Though I had the Knife, and I'd like to think I didn't reach crazy bitch levels of behaviour, but . . .'

He raised his head and studied her. 'Well, you're only part-Few, though. Maybe that makes a difference?'

'Jake's touched the Knife too, but the worst that happened to him happened *before* he ever touched it. Or at least, that's what I thought . . .' Cassie's breathing quickened. What had her friends got themselves embroiled in? What if the Knife made Jake's vengeful nature even worse?

Richard was reading the pages closely again. He remained silent for a few more minutes, occasionally sighing deeply. Then he shuffled the papers into a neat pile, took a breath, and stood up quite sharply.

'I don't know. I don't really know what to make of all this. But, Cassie, speaking of Keiko . . . Listen to me.' He turned.

He was very close. *Alarmingly* close. Cassie wanted to take a step back but found she couldn't. There was a look on his face, almost pleading, and he was nibbling the corner of his lip in a way that made Cassie's heart pound. He lifted his hands.

Oh God, she thought. Is he going to try and kiss me again? Please don't let him try and kiss me. Not right now, too confusing, too complicated—

'Cassie, I—'

'Hold on!' She raised a warning finger to his face, and he started back. But instead of moving away, her body took over. Instead of pushing him away, she found herself grabbing his head in two hands, pulling him to her, pressing her lips to his and . . .

Kissing *him*.

Richard was shocked only for a moment; then he was responding with enthusiasm, deepening the kiss. She moved her tongue to find his, and he gave a little groan of lust. He wasn't the only one, she thought, pulling him closer. Her fingers raked slowly, luxuriantly through his silky hair, breathing in deeply through her nose, smelling the woody, warm scent of his skin . . .

Bloody hell!

Pulling back, she wobbled, getting her breath and her composure back. He looked in much the same state.

'Well.' She put a hand to her chest, and did her best to make a joke of it. 'I, uh, I thought we should just . . . get that out of the way.'

Something flitted across his face – hurt, disappointment? – but then the shutters were down again.

'Fair enough, beautiful,' he retorted, winking. But there was no mirth in his voice.

She was hopelessly confused now, more about herself than about him. 'Richard, I'm sorry. Um, were you going to tell me something?'

'I'm not. Not sorry, I mean.' He sounded over-bright now, like he always did in defensive mode. 'And actually, it's late. Let's leave it. We should get some sleep, think this over. It's a lot to take in.' He stopped and pointed to the printed pages, as though he was concerned she might have thought he meant something else. 'Shall I see you in the morning?'

'Um, OK.' Cassie was lost for words as she watched him walk out of the room and close the door.

She *was* sorry. She'd just done something stupid. So very, unbelievably stupid. Still – had she misread him completely? He'd looked almost upset, like this meant more to him than she thought . . .

Cassie shook her head violently. She couldn't afford to worry about someone else on top of Ranjit – feel something for anyone else.

She had to focus.

What had Ranjit been looking for? Maybe she should get some sleep and this would all make more sense in the morning. But, turning back to the pages that detailed the artefacts, she stared at them once again.

The Pendant may, for a spell of time, draw the Spirit from its Host.

Oh. God.
She flipped a sheet of paper.

The Knife may Sever the connection between Spirit and Host. Only this Knife, or Death itself, may break the Bond.

Cassie blinked. What had Ranjit said to her, at the start of term?

I know a way for us to be together. We will be together, I promise you that!

That didn't have to mean anything sinister. It didn't. But it was more than that. Something else was at the edge of her mind, something she didn't want to remember, but something she had to. Come *on*, Cassie! She tugged at her hair, trying to wrench the memory free. And then, she did remember.

Ranjit's last hyper, frantic phone call.

I know how, now. How to heal old wounds.

BREAK OLD TIES!

A cold shiver of dread ran down her spine. Ranjit had asked her about the Knife. And the symbol he'd photographed at Hagia Sophia: she was almost certain it bore a distinct similarity to that engraving of the symbol under which the Pendant supposedly lay. Had he found it, then?

All at once, it hit her. She knew, very suddenly and sickeningly, what had been missing from Sir Alric's study that day. Darke had been so distracted, so nervous, and he'd turned his own office upside down looking for something. Yes, something had been missing. That pale, ornate jade vase, the one that reflected the light so prettily. A vase? *No.*

The Urn.

Sir Alric must have found the Urn, and where better to hide it than in plain sight? Cassie gulped hard. The Urn, which could contain and preserve a spirit indefinitely . . .

Cassandra, NO! It can't be . . . Absolutely not. We must walk away NOW!

'Break old ties . . .' Cassie whispered, shock making her

232

voice quiver. 'Oh my God. Ranjit.' She shut her eyes, fear thrilling into her bones. *What were you planning?*

What have you done?

CHAPTER TWENTY-THREE

Cassie was good at this. And so she should be. From being the Cranlake Crescent insomniac skulker, she'd slipped naturally and easily into the same role at the Darke Academy. Yes, the school sneak. Why not? Silent and alone, she prowled the halls once more. Though she was never entirely alone, of course. Estelle's dissent was almost impossible for Cassie to ignore, but she was trying her level best.

Cassandra, you must listen to me. This is a mistake of magnificent proportion. We must stay as far away from this plot as we can . . . he means to separate us . . . Cassandra, please . . . !

Cassie took a deep breath and pushed the spirit's voice as far back in her mind as she could. There was no way she was turning back. If she'd worked this out right, if Ranjit had decoded the Few manuscript, or at least part of it, and was trying to locate the artefacts, then there was no doubt at all that Sir Alric Darke had found it out by now too. She didn't have a choice: she had to search his office, try and find out what he knew, how close he was coming to Ranjit.

There was no other movement at all as Cassie crept along the darkened corridors or dodged the shadows of the filigree lamps. Even Marat was lying low, perhaps satisfied with one corpse for now and not in need of intrigue or spying. Outside Sir Alric's office Cassie paused, ears alert for any sound. Close by, there was only the rustle of a cat in the garden, the frightened squeak of a mouse, and far in the distance the city sounds of traffic and horns and faraway music, drifting across the quiet Bosphorus.

The door was locked, of course. This time she couldn't pick the lock, having no gold hairpin borrowed from Isabella as she'd had on prior occasions, but that wasn't problem now. Despite Estelle's increasing protests, she felt confident enough in her ability to control the bizarre, invisible power she had acquired with her broken induction ceremony. It was pretty straightforward to focus it on the lock, to feel the mechanism's keyhole start to shift, glowing through the red filter of her vision. Curiously, she stretched out a hand, but that wasn't necessary – she could feel the incandescent heat of the lock at her fingertips, stinging her skin. Clenching her fist and concentrating harder, the lock clicked open with a satisfying *thunk*.

Smiling, Cassie pushed open the door. The office was in semi-darkness, but there was the light of the moon, and she moved quickly across the room to switch on that pretty desk lamp. Letting the red fade from her eyes as they adjusted to the dim light, she turned a slow circle, examining the room.

It wasn't as if she was going to steal anything – she wouldn't take anything she didn't have a right to – but seeing as he was clearly not telling the Few everything, she'd have to figure things out for herself. She had a sense of honour, after all. Unlike Sir Alric Darke, she thought bitterly.

But he did protect you, he did save you from the Council, whispered a small inner voice that wasn't Estelle's. Maybe there's a reason he's hiding things?

That was her conscience, presumably. Cassie chose to ignore it. Can't afford you any more, she thought. Instead she stood in the centre of the room, glaring around as if her eyes could bore a hole in the wall. Maybe she should try it? No. She'd have to do this the old-fashioned way. She began to hunt through drawers and cabinets.

Her search was methodical, systematic, thorough. When she'd finished with the most obvious places, she began to pull books from the shelves, one by one. She was on the third shelf down when she felt it.

'Ow!'

It was like electricity, the little jolt of power that surged into her finger. Cassie jumped back, startled, then reached up to that point on the bookshelves again, bumping her fingertip along the spines until she felt that little jolt once again.

Excitement rising inside her, mingling with trepidation, she pulled books from the shelf and piled them on the floor. There, behind them, a small safe was set into the wall.

Wow, she was getting good at this.

No, Cassandra, we mustn't . . .

'Yes, Estelle,' Cassie muttered, concentrating hard. It was the work of moments this time to manipulate the mechanisms of the safe's locks, and when she swung open the heavy door and reached inside, she found the cavity was quite deep. Deep enough to hold a green leather folder, old and worn, with that familiar Few symbol embossed in gold on its cover.

Fascinated, she stroked its cover, then sat down in Sir Alric's chair and laid it on his desk beneath the glow of the ornate lamp.

With a deep breath, she opened it, and then froze.

These were no thin, laser-printed pages; this was the original manuscript. Not only did Darke have the pages she'd found on Ranjit's computer – and the illustrations were inked in beautiful colours, the engravings on the real thing being even more elaborate and beautiful – but he had the *second half* of the manuscript, too. Cassie swallowed hard, and then quickly began to read.

Here were the things that hadn't been explained. Of course, the Elders had hidden the two parts separately, so afraid were they of the artefacts being discovered. A reasonable precaution, but pretty pointless in the days of computerised archives and instantly accessible information. Smart they might have been, those Elders, but they hadn't foreseen the internet . . . Cassie couldn't help smiling bitterly. The manuscript could never have been found by an ordinary researching historian, she'd bet her life on that, but a modern Few, technically literate, who knew what he was looking for? Hardly a problem at all.

Cassie lifted the bound pages delicately, laying each one down with care. Yes, here in the second part of the manuscript was the precise location of the Pendant: a basilica in the Hagia Sophia. Ranjit's having only the first part of the document obviously meant he hadn't known its location though; he could been searching all over Istanbul for the symbol that was mentioned in his part of the manuscript, and perhaps it had been sheer bloody luck that he'd spotted the carved emblem that day on their school trip. In any case, Ranjit must have, at some point, had this original of the first half in his possession. How else could he have scanned the pages and saved them on his computer? He may have been mysterious but Ranjit was also fiercely intelligent. The scans must have been a precaution. In case . . . in case someone like Sir Alric came snooping around and took them . . .

That small pleasure of Ranjit getting one up on Darke died almost immediately. Cassie's mind whirled. If Sir Alric had the whole manuscript, both parts, then it was always possible that he had also got to the Pendant first.

'Maybe Ranjit was too late?' Cassie mumbled, half hoping but not fully believing. She stared at the new page she'd turned, so smooth and yellowed by age. As her eyes skimmed the script, her heart plummeted to the furthest depths of her chest.

'Oh, Ranjit. Oh, my God,' she whispered.

These artefacts must never be actively sought by
the Few, lest the worst of their nature
be brought out in the finder. The first
of our kind to once again lay hands upon
these items will face a devastating result.

'These artefacts must never be actively sought . . .' Cassie couldn't help but read the words aloud, her eyes wide with horror.

The worst of their nature?

She felt her fingers tense with rage and fear as she started at the details. Of course, it would have to be the first contact; after that it would be rendered safe once more. After all, the Elders would probably want the artefacts back, wouldn't they? They'd have to be able to touch the artefacts themselves, once the poor unsuspecting thief had lost their marbles . . .

Cassie flattened her hands against the page, almost trying not to see the spidery script. There was no way round it. The first person to touch Pendant, Knife or Urn would change – and it definitely didn't sound like it was for the better.

It explained everything, of course. Keiko had been no Pollyanna, but the Knife had given her a new, psychopathic hatred and violence. She'd been out of her mind when she tried to kill Cassie. That somehow made her feel even worse about the Japanese girl's terrible death.

Hurriedly Cassie turned more pages, handling the heavy vellum with great care. She couldn't help feeling respectful of the manuscript's age, even as she wanted to rip the damned thing into tiny pieces.

And there it was: the Urn's location. Cassie couldn't help gulping hard and shoving the chair back, as if she could distance herself physically from what this meant.

The Yucatán . . .

Patrick's words from all those weeks ago came back to her with a horrible jolt.

Erik was killed . . . in a landslide . . . I always wondered what they were looking for, out there in the Yucatán.

But Sir Alric never said . . .

Of course he didn't: it was a secret project. A top-secret, mysterious, Few-related project, entrusted only to the reliable, honourable Erik Ragnarsson. Oh Lord. They must have found the Urn. And something terrible had happened to Erik. But then it was entirely possible that Erik had been first to touch their find. Maybe Erik had

241

been cursed in Sir Alric's place.

Cassie didn't want to think about it. What had happened to him? Only he and Sir Alric had been there. Erik was Few. He'd touched the Urn, been struck with the curse . . . and then what? A landslide, and Erik dead, or so Sir Alric said. What a convenient landslide. Oh God . . .

No matter how much Cassie tried not to think about it, she knew one devastating fact was almost certain. That Ranjit had no idea of this. No idea about what might happen if he was the first to touch an artefact.

He couldn't have if he hadn't seen the other half of this manuscript. Ranjit had more than likely gone blindly in search of the Pendant, thinking it could save his relationship with her, without a clue about the consequences. Or at least not the consequences for himself . . .

Then Cassie remembered the missing Urn, its sudden disappearance from the very office in which she now sat. There was every chance it was Ranjit who had taken it, but Erik's sacrifice must mean that the Urn was safe to touch. The Pendant, however, was a different story.

And now Ranjit had disappeared.

Could Sir Alric have been using him too? But what about the others – Mikhail, Yusuf? What was he covering up? Was his mention of Jake just a diversion, a way to throw her off the scent?

Cassie's breath became ragged as the horror of all the possibilities began to assail her mind. She had to get out of there, and fast. Covering her tracks as best she could, Cassie replaced the manuscript, spun the dial to lock the vault and replaced the books on the shelf, her head spinning.

We must take great care, my dear . . . please, please be reasonable . . . there may be nothing we can do . . . we shouldn't continue to pursue this . . . PLEASE!

Maybe there is nothing to be done, Cassie thought. But if there was any chance that Ranjit was still alive, she had to find him. She had to try and help him.

CHAPTER TWENTY-FOUR

As she quietly pulled the office door shut, Cassie was acutely aware that she *really* did not want to run into anyone on her way back to her room: there was potential for far too many awkward questions, and not many answers she could give. Edging into the next corridor she took a breath, listening for any footstep, preparing to make a dash for it.

Then her ringtone shrieked, slicing through the silence.

Swearing, Cassie fumbled in her pocket, almost dropping the phone as she dragged it out.

'Shut up,' she hissed wildly, silencing it at last. Leaning back against the wall, trying to breathe without a high note of panic, she peered at the illuminated caller ID.

Richard H-J

She was goggling at that, wondering what he wanted at this time of night, when something moved at the corner of her eye. Jerking her head round, she went absolutely still, senses pricked.

At the end of the passageway. Someone, there. They'd retreated into the shadows; maybe even ducked round the corner. Marat?

No, she decided. The figure was too light on its feet, had moved too fast.

But not half as fast as she could.

Angry, her senses clicking smoothly into high alert, Cassie sprinted after the shadow.

Whoever it was, they were a fast mover. When she reached the corner it was already running for the stairs, vaulting over the banisters and halfway down the first flight. Cassie reached the top of the stairs just as it vanished into the next bedroom corridor.

With a growl she leaped over the banisters in pursuit; no time for using the steps. She dashed into the corridor and caught the shadow's edge as it bolted round a corner. He wouldn't get away. He, she, *it* wouldn't get away. Cassie put on speed, skidding into the next passageway, then sprang in a single leap down the next flight of stairs. She bounced off the far wall and recovered her footing, just in time to see the figure dodge into a bedroom and close the door – but quietly, as if he thought he'd escaped detection.

She halted, smiling grimly, then walked to the room where the shadow had vanished. Raising her fist to rap on the wood, she stopped short, breath stuck in her windpipe.

ALICE PRITCHARD

Alice. Alice, who hadn't shared a room since the death of her roommate Keiko in the autumn term. Alice, who was now permitted a room alone for the rest of her school career, unless she wished to share.

And now she did. Because Isabella had moved in.

So who was the shadowy prowler? Alice? Isabella? That didn't make sense.

Cassie felt suddenly sick. There was one other person she knew who liked to prowl the school corridors. One person who held a grudge that wouldn't go away. Someone else who'd once been a scholarship student, but not any more. Someone who shouldn't even be here . . .

Anger filling her as the shock drained away, Cassie hammered on the door. In less than two seconds, it was flung open.

Isabella's face was stony, her lips compressed. She looked at Cassie with what seemed like all the defiance in her soul, and that was a lot. For a fleeting moment Cassie wondered if she'd even get past the girl; then her eye was caught by a figure behind Isabella, and she glared over her shoulder.

Tall, rangy, crop-haired, and a good bit colder-eyed than he used to be. He didn't smile, but nor did he avert his eyes. A war of emotions rattled through Cassie's mind. It was unexpectedly good to see the American boy, despite it all. But all the deception, the unknown motivations, the resentment in his gaze . . .

'I knew it,' she spat. 'Jake Johnson.'

Isabella said nothing, but Cassie could her breathing hard, and she still barred the doorway like a bodyguard. There was no point trying to play the Few card and bully her way into the room; that wouldn't cut any ice with these two.

Cassie made a big effort to control her dangerous temper. After all, they'd been friends once, and they'd faced a lot together; whatever had come between them, she was glad he was all right. Oddly glad, too, to see him back with Isabella. Breathing out slowly, Cassie shrugged. She didn't want a fight.

'Look,' she sighed, 'just tell me what's going on, please? Where's Alice?'

The charge of tension seemed to leak from the air like grounded electricity. With a confrontation off the cards, Isabella looked a little less sure of herself. 'She's gone to

Ankara for the weekend. Her uncle works there. Cassie, I can't tell you everything but I can explain what's—'

'No,' Jake interrupted, putting his hands on her shoulders and moving her gently aside. 'I'll tell her.'

Cassie eyed him as she stepped into the room. 'Have you got the Knife, Jake?'

'Who wants to know? You, or Estelle?'

She kept hold of her temper, sighing deeply. 'We're the same, Jake; get used to it. You haven't answered my question. Have you got the Knife? Has Ranjit been in touch about it?'

'What?' Isabella looked baffled.

Jake gave his girlfriend a wary glance and said hastily, 'I'm here because of Isabella. I'm here because I love her and I couldn't stay away, OK?'

Cassie eyed him sceptically. 'Right. So why have you been following me?'

'Like you used to followed me?' he retorted. 'It isn't any of your business, Cassie. I'm just glad Isabella's seen the light about you.'

'Jake, no!' protested Isabella. She looked beseechingly at Cassie. 'I meant it: this is only a breathing space. Cassie and I both needed time to ourselves, Jake, that's all. Look, Cassie, I'm sorry I lied to you. I couldn't tell you, and I needed to be with him. You have to understand.'

Cassie took a deep breath. It hurt, that was true, but she *did* understand. Besides, it wasn't as if she'd had no secrets from Isabella.

'Yeah. Yes, course I do, Isabella. But how's he been coming and going? Jake shouldn't be able to get into the Academy.'

'I found somebody in the city who'd clone my Academy pass.' Isabella looked a little sheepish. 'It was easier than I thought it would be. Someone at the Book Bazaar did it: replaced my photo and my name with Jake's – not his real name, obviously. He used a fake one. The boatmen aren't all that interested anyway; so long as they see a pass they don't check too closely.'

'I pull a hat down over my head when I get on or off the boat,' added Jake. 'Nobody takes any notice of me. The other kids probably assume I'm a gardener or a cleaner.' There was a distinct tinge of old bitterness in his tone.

Isabella slipped an arm round his waist. 'Cassie, you must believe Jake has had nothing to do with those . . . killings,' she pleaded.

Cassie was silent for a long moment, her thoughts going in horrible directions.

'She's right,' said Jake. 'It doesn't matter to me what you think, but for what it's worth, I had nothing to do with those deaths. Or Ranjit's disappearance.'

'No,' Cassie said slowly. 'I believe you.'

'Have you heard anything from him?' he asked. 'Ranjit?'

Cassie paused, trying to contain the fear and worry at the very mention of him. 'As you said. It's none of your business.'

There was an awkward silence for several seconds, but Cassie didn't regret snapping. She was thinking too hard, wondering what to do.

'Did it occur to you that Ranjit's body hasn't turned up,' asked Jake softly, 'because he's the one doing the killing?'

'What? How dare you!' She took an abrupt step backwards. Her shock at his suggestion was heightened by the fact that, somewhere very deep down, she may have had the same thought herself . . .

'He's evil, Cassie. I know how you feel about him and I'm sorry, but *everything* points to him. With Jess, and with the others now too. Look, he led you on, got you to trust him, but didn't he always let you down when it counted?'

She found she didn't trust her voice. Not to answer that question, anyway. Resolutely she ignored it.

'Ranjit wanted something from you,' she told Jake coldly. 'Are you quite sure he hasn't been in touch?'

'I haven't seen him since I got to Istanbul, Cassie. Yeah,

he suggested a meeting, some crap about offering me information, but it doesn't matter because it didn't happen. He didn't show. I never really thought he would; who'd trust Ranjit Singh?' he sneered. 'I'm here because of Jess, but I'm here for Isabella too.'

Isabella pressed even closer to him and squeezed his hand.

'I don't give a shit about Ranjit Singh,' he went on. 'And you know what? I wish I *had* seen him, because I'd love to get my hands on him. Maybe even more than you. But I haven't, and I've got nothing to do with him going missing.'

I WILL fix this! She couldn't get Ranjit's excited voice out of her head. *Cassie, I WILL fix this . . . I know how, now . . . Break old ties . . . Break old ties!*

'Fine,' she said softly.

'You believe me?'

'*Yes.*' She took a deep breath. 'Yes. Yes, I do believe you.'

The beep from her phone made her jump, eyes so wide that Jake frowned in curiosity. 'What?'

Blinking, she tugged the phone urgently out of her pocket and stared at it. 'Damn it,' she whispered quickly. 'Richard – I had a call. I totally forgot. He's left a message.'

Jake turned away with a show of contempt, but Isabella

251

watched her anxiously as she held the phone to her ear.

'Cassie, what is it? What's wrong?'

Cassie held a finger to her lips as she listened to the message, but she knew she must be going pale. She could feel the blood draining from her face, and by the time Richard's recorded message clicked dead, she was dizzy. She couldn't press the disconnect button, just lowered her hand to her side so that she could still hear the distant prissy voicemail: '. . . *to save, press two. To delete, press three . . .*'

'Cassie?'

Something was stuck in her throat. She coughed. 'Richard. He's . . . he says he's heard from Ranjit.'

Jake spun round, excitement in his eyes. 'So let's go find the little bastard! He can take us to Ran—'

'He's gone to meet him. Wants me to come and meet them.' Cassie felt like her voice was coming from someone else.

'What?' Jake prompted. 'Where?'

'Hagia Sophia.' Cassie finally killed the voicemail with her thumb and frantically pressed Richard's speed-dial button. 'Answer. Please, please. *Answer!*' Her voice was rising close to hysteria.

If Ranjit was alive, if he was hanging around the Hagia Sophia, then there was every possibility that he could have found the Pendant before Sir Alric. And if he'd found the Pendant before Sir Alric then he could be . . . dangerous.

It seemed as if no one was breathing when she finally snapped her phone shut, an awful fear tightening her throat.

'Switched off,' she whispered. 'Richard's switched off his phone. And he's going to meet Ranjit. Alone.'

CHAPTER TWENTY-FIVE

'He'll be fine.' Isabella came to Cassie to console her, resting a hand on her arm, her brows knitted in confusion at Cassie's reaction. 'Richard always is. He is a . . . a survivor, yes?'

'He's a snake,' growled Jake.

'I don't understand! It's a good thing that Ranjit's OK, right?' exclaimed Isabella. 'Cassie?'

'It's too complicated to explain.' Cassie shook her head. 'Listen, Richard's in trouble. Serious, serious trouble. You've got to help me.'

Isabella blinked. 'Since when have you been so worried about Richard? I thought you—'

'I know, I know, never mind all that. I don't want him to get hurt. Please help?'

'Of course we—'

'I mean, the only way you *can*.' Fear made her voice

hard. 'Isabella, I think I'm going to have to fight Ranjit. I need to be strong enough.'

Isabella took a sharp breath, and a step closer to Jake.

'No friggin' *way*,' he snapped, seizing Isabella's hand and pulling her back towards him.

'You'd rather see Richard die?' barked Cassie.

'Do *not* make me answer that one.'

'Ranjit may be under a curse,' she said, her teeth clenched, her voice low, dangerous. 'There's a . . . a Pendant. It's . . . special. If he's found it, he may not be himself, OK? He won't hold back! I need to be stronger, *damn it*! I need to feed.'

Isabella bit her lip, seeming to hesitate, and then took a step forward, but Jake yanked her behind him. 'No, Isabella!'

Cassie's jaw tightened. 'Stay out of it, Jake!'

'No way. Are you kidding me? *Over my dead body!*'

Oh, don't tempt me . . . Cassie took deep, slow breaths, trying to stop the room turning red. Fists balled up, she took a pace towards Jake, and saw his hand grab at something in his belt. A knife-hilt. *The* Knife.

Her eyes narrowed and her breath hissed through her teeth. He'd lifted his T-shirt slightly and she could see the hilt clearly now, pressed against his hard stomach muscles. Its mythical creatures were dead, unmoving, lifeless: it was nothing but a carving. Violent resentment surged through her.

'That isn't yours,' she hissed. 'You have no right to it. None!'

'Still sharp, though,' he growled.

Cassie couldn't remember when she had last breathed. Now she took a great lungful of air, shaking her head, desperately clearing her vision of its scarlet filter. 'No,' she murmured. 'No . . .'

We should take him, my darling! Don't tell me no!

No! she snapped back in her mind. Shut up, Estelle!

Control yourself, Cassie . . . For all his myriad faults, Sir Alric had been right on that. And she must. She *must*. This was *Jake*, for God's sake!

She shut her eyes hard. 'We haven't got time for this.'

Jake eyed her warily for a long time before he spoke. 'Fine. I agree.' His hand moved a little further from the hilt. He gave Isabella a sidelong, fierce glance. 'So feed on me.'

Cassie started. 'What?'

'Jake, no!' exclaimed Isabella.

'Why not? You've done it, right? You say it's safe. So what have I got to be scared of? If you've been telling me the truth.' He turned back to Cassie. 'I get it. You need to be strong. So come on. Feed on me.'

She nodded, slowly at first, then more vigorously. 'I haven't got time to argue. You'll do.' She stepped swiftly up to him, seized his arms and turned his wrists up to face her.

'Could you have put that a little more tactfully?' He was attempting a wry smile, but without much luck, and he was so tense she could feel the sinews standing out against his muscles.

She smiled up into his nervous eyes, pitiless. He'd kept her from her prey, the interfering mortal; he could damn well stand in without a fuss.

. . . Something deep inside her quailed and shivered. What was she *thinking*?

But she was too hungry, too afraid, too desperate to worry. She slapped the small voice of her conscience away and tightened her grip on Jake's wrists, thumbs finding his veins. She was aware of Isabella's frightened breathing, her small nervous movements as she glanced anxiously from Jake to Cassie and back, but Cassie took no notice. Jake sucked in a breath as she focused, found his life, and began to feed.

His essence roared into her. He'd been working out, she thought with an amused layer of her mind. He was strong, fit, and more than that, he had a powerful will. The boy was determined. And she was soaking it all up, the life of him thrilling into her, racing through her veins.

Jake stumbled a little. She was aware of her fingers tight as iron bands around his wrists, her thumbs digging hard into his skin. Veins bulged at his temple, stood out against the tanned skin of his arms, and his face was drained by shock. Isabella was tugging at her sleeve.

'Cassie, you need to stop.'

No. No we mustn't stop! Not yet!

'CASSIE!'

Cassie let him go with an angry cry. In front of her Jake wobbled wildly, grabbed for the wall, and righted himself.

'Holy crap.' He could speak before Cassie could.

She stood rigid, letting life-energy fizz into her fingertips, her scalp, the soles of her feet.

'You . . . are *never* . . . feeding off my girl again.'

Says who? she wanted to snarl. Just as well she couldn't speak yet.

Jake's arm, she noticed, was tight around Isabella's shoulders. The gesture looked protective, but Cassie could tell Isabella was actually supporting her boyfriend. He was still unsteady on his pins, she realised, a little shocked at the frisson of pleasure she took from that.

'I'm going,' she said with disdain. 'I've stayed too long already. Thanks, Jake.'

'Wait!'

She'd already flung open the door, but his voice had enough urgency to stop her. She glanced over her shoulder with irritation.

Jake looked steadier, and already the colour was seeping back into his face. 'I'm coming with you.'

'No. Really. You're not.' She sighed. 'You'll get in the way.'

'Oh, get over yourself. And while you're at it, get over Ranjit.' He glared at her.

Cassie scowled. 'You're not coming.'

'This theory of yours, about the Pendant. What is it, a wild guess?' He twisted his lip in a cynical smirk. 'You don't have any proof, do you, Cassie? Thought not. So Ranjit might not be under a spell. Ranjit might just be doing what comes naturally. Either way, you can't handle him.'

Cassie gave a bark of incredulous laughter. 'I'm sorry?'

'And I'm serious. I always knew there was something bad about Ranjit, whether it's down to some curse or not. If he's not in control of himself, he won't hold back from hurting you. I could understand that you needed feeding, to be the best you can be – but you need to understand that you'll need back-up. Frankly, even if he knows what he's doing, I can't imagine why you'd trust him. It's not like he gives a damn. I'm pretty sure he'd kill you as soon as look at you.'

'No, he wouldn't!'

'Uh-huh. Because he's proved his love on so many occasions.'

'Shut up.' Cassie reddened.

'You, on the other hand, won't be able to hurt *him*. Not in the final analysis. You won't so much as blacken one beautiful eye of his.' Jake smirked again, folding his arms. 'Go on and tell me I'm wrong.'

She breathed hard, wordless, incapable of arguing with that. At last she twisted her mouth into a sneer. 'Fine, come on then. It's your funeral.'

'Now just wait a minute!' Isabella flung herself between them. 'I don't like this talk of anyone's *funeral*. And you two are quite likely to turn on each other! I'll come too.'

Groaning, Cassie tore at her hair. 'I *haven't got* another minute! Jake, tell her. She's not coming, no way!'

'Cassie's right, baby,' agreed Jake. 'You can't come, not this time. Please, we don't have time. Just trust me, do this for me,' He pushed Isabella gently but firmly back into the room. 'I love you.' The girl opened her mouth to argue at the top of her considerable voice, but this stopped her. She nodded silently.

Trying to ignore the exchange, Cassie turned and briskly began to walk from the room. After a moment, she broke into a run, but Jake was at her heels.

She did her best to outrun him, leave him behind, but he wasn't having it. He was at her heel through the dark passageways, down the stairs and out through the courtyard. At the top of the great flight of entrance stairs Cassie halted and flung out an arm. Jake collided with it.

'Oof! What?'

'Give me the Knife.' She turned to face him.

'No.'

'It's mine. It's *ours*,' she corrected herself.

'See, you talk like that and you scare me. Forget it, I'm not giving it to you.'

'You'll regret it. You've no idea how to use it. *None*.'

'I know better than you think. And I told you, it works just fine without your supernatural little paws on it.'

In the moonlight they stood for seconds more, facing one another, livid. It was Cassie, looking at her watch, who turned away first.

'No time,' she snapped. 'Not now. You can hotwire an engine?'

'Course.' There was a distinct grin in his voice – partly, she thought sourly, from his small victory.

'Good. So you can actually make yourself useful.' She sprinted for the jetty. 'We're going to liberate a speedboat.'

CHAPTER TWENTY-SIX

Jake was still close behind Cassie as she bolted through the city streets. The buildings of Sultanahmet were tall, the streets and alleyways tortuously winding, but Hagia Sophia dominated everything, floodlit like a gigantic golden jewel, its dome and minarets towering above the city streets. They couldn't miss it. Cassie leaped a railing and raced across parkland towards it. Constantly she was aware of the Knife in Jake's possession, alive and calling out to her, but she didn't let it distract her.

She'd get it later.

Both of them slowed as they approached the massive steps, careful now, senses alert. Cassie could hear Jake breathing hard. He'd kept up with her, certainly, but despite all the workouts he still couldn't run so far or so fast. That was worth knowing.

No, stop it, Cassie!

'Where do we start?' muttered Jake, stopping beside her to catch his breath.

Cassie rested a hand on a gilded pillar, reaching out with her senses, trying to think every part of herself into this place. Yes, where? She should know. She *could* know, if she could only feel it . . .

Where would HE go, Cassandra? Think as he does, my darling! We must learn to out-think him!

All very well, she thought dryly, but Ranjit might not exactly be thinking like his usual self. She was sorely tempted to call Richard's name, but she knew that was a temptation she had to resist. She knew by instinct that he wouldn't reply, not now. But Ranjit might.

The mosque was huge. As they walked silently through its massive arched doors, even now Cassie was dazzled by its splendid beauty. Just for seconds, though. Splendour she was used to, now. She was impressed, but not intimidated. Jake, though: he was different. She could sense his awe. He positively reeked of it. She let a little smile flicker across her face.

'Do you hear anything?' he whispered.

She went still, reaching out with her senses. 'Yes. Not in here.' She turned sharply to the south-west. 'Follow me.'

Mausoleums stood to the side of the mosque, and

Cassie kept to the shadows, but she was in a hurry now. She didn't so much hear something as feel it. The central tomb was the one she wanted: a squat, domed building with a vaulted portico. Silently and swiftly, she ran up the stone steps and inside the mausoleum.

It was breathtaking. Eight huge arches, elaborately tiled, covered in mosaics and inscriptions, towered above the silent sarcophagi. The stone and the space smelled of centuries, and the silence echoed with ghosts. Shadows and ghosts. Cassie realised she wasn't breathing as she listened intently. Carefully, she stepped inside. She stared, but not at the majesty of the architecture.

He was there, standing before the largest sarcophagus. Ranjit.

He was looking straight at her but he didn't seem to see her. His eyes were red from corner to corner and he was entirely motionless.

The sight of him, after so long, brought Cassie to a standstill as well. His fists were clenched tightly, and she could see the hairs standing up on his arms, as if he was electrified. At his feet, prone and barely conscious, lay Richard.

Cassie froze, riveted with horrified fascination, as Jake stopped dead at her side. Ranjit looked ferociously, vibrantly alive. He turned to them finally with a twitch in his mad face, a hint of recognition, and he smiled, but it was not a nice one.

'Ah! This is wonderful. My friends!'

'Ranjit, listen to me—'

He cut her off as if she hadn't spoken. 'Jake has brought me the Knife after all! I'm *so* very sorry I missed our original rendezvous; I got a bit, uh, caught up!' He laughed wildly. 'Yes, Cassie, we had an appointment, Jake and I. He wanted to know all about Jess; I wanted the Knife. A pretty good trade, don't you think? But I am sorry, Jake. I was unavoidably delayed.'

'Ranjit,' she cried, fear making her shrill. 'This isn't you!'

'That's where you're wrong, Cassie; this is more me than ever! Don't you see? I've done all this for you! Getting the Urn from Sir Alric's office was easy. He assumed nobody else was aware of its power but . . .' His eyes darted, as though his mind was racing. 'The Knife, well, I'd hoped I'd get it sooner, but it's here now, isn't it, my friends. But I knew I had to find the Pendant before I could really help you, and I did! I've got it. I told you, didn't I? I told you I'd fix everything! And I know you'll be grateful, Cassie. I know it.'

Grateful? Cassandra, we must go NOW!

'Ranjit, stop this!' she shouted, furious and afraid. Her

voice echoed over the hard surfaces of the mausoleum.

'But I killed them for *you!*' he cried. 'The ones who got you into this mess! I'm going through them, one by one, those who were at your ceremony. They forced you to host Estelle's spirit. But it's OK. I can get her out of you. I can get her out, and I can punish the ones who did this! My *gift* to you, my love! Isn't it magnificent? My gift: your life back. And their lives – I give you those, too!'

Cassie was reeling. 'I didn't want them!' she screamed.

He wasn't even listening. Instead he pointed to a bulging canvas bag that lay on the floor, the pale edge of the jade Urn just showing at the open flap. 'I have all three of the Eldest's creations, now that Jake's come along, now that he's brought the Knife to me. But fair's fair! I wouldn't deprive him of our deal, I wouldn't withhold what I promised! That wouldn't be like me, would it, Cassie?'

'Ranjit! *None of this* is like you! It's the curse, the—'

'Now Jake can have his answers. And he'll be glad of this . . .' he gestured to Richard, still lying at Ranjit's feet, his eyes widening in panic.

'Ranjit. No . . .' he said, weakly.

'. . . when I tell him that it was Richard here who delayed me the night Jess was killed,' Ranjit continued, ignoring Richard's protest. 'And trust me, it was very much deliberate.'

Cassie felt like her heart had stopped – and Jake was like cold stone beside her. She couldn't even hear him breathing.

Ranjit's eyes seemed to look past them once more. 'Yes. Yes, Cassie, I loved her once too, like I love you now. I was too late, too late to get to her because this little weasel kept me back while Keiko and Katerina hunted her down in the forest. Let's be honest, Jess never stood a chance.' He focused back on them. 'But now you do, my love.'

Cassie wasn't aware of Jake moving, only of a blur that flew past her and leaped towards the sarcophagus. The Knife was in his hand and he was screaming, incomprehensibly.

Ranjit's head turned, almost imperceptibly, his mad grin unchanged. He looked quite unconcerned, but as if in slow motion Cassie saw one fist flash out, striking Jake with a fluid, lethal grace. Jake grunted with pain as he was flung like a rag across the floor of the tomb, then slammed into a pillar. Cassie saw it all, heard it all, as if she was watching some crazy piece of theatre, and through a curtain too.

Then she heard the terrible crack as Jake's skull broke. And she screamed.

'Ranjit, NO!'

She and Ranjit both stared at Jake's limp body, heaped untidily on the floor, but Ranjit's red eyes still held no human expression at all. Slowly he turned back to Richard, and stretched out a hand. As Ranjit grabbed Richard's shirt, his chest arched up, head lolling, and a small rattling whimper came from his lips. He was slipping out of consciousness again . . .

Rage crept up Cassie's spine, filling her, and suddenly the beautiful Iznik tiles of the tomb were purple-red in her vision. Snarling, she clenched her fists and focused her fury, a crackling aura beyond her body, and lashed it at Ranjit.

This time he took notice, head snapping up just too late. As her power hit him he was thrown back, banging into another pillar. He roared, lunging back towards Richard like an animal, and Cassie hit him harder, flinging Ranjit into the air.

He landed on his feet like a tiger. His eyes boiled as they focused on her, the light mad with passion and rage.

'You're protecting *him*?' Ranjit's voice was horrible, hissing through peeled-back lips. 'He's the one who got you into this mess! He's the reason we're apart! I'm the one who's *helping* you, Cassie!'

'Get away from him. From both of them!' Cassie knew

her own voice was shaking, but with fear or fury even she didn't know.

Ranjit threw back his head and let rip a hideous, shrieking laugh. 'God, it's so ironic! You're defending Jakey too!'

'Ranjit, get a grip.' She snarled it in a low voice, desperate to get through to him. 'This isn't *you!*'

'I told you, it's more me than ever, sweetheart.' He laughed again, head falling forward as he leered at her, and she saw something swing free from his black T-shirt. A glowing green thing on a silver chain.

Riveted with horror, she stared at it, swinging gently, gleaming. Dawn was sending a creeping light into the vast tomb, encroaching on the shadows around the eight arches, and she could see the jade very well. It was a plain circle, but it moved, squirmed, *lived*. She knew if she looked closer she'd recognise the creatures carved into it. They'd be the same ones that lived and squirmed on the knife-hilt in Jake's inert hand. The same ones she'd seen in the engraving on the manuscript.

'Ranjit,' she pleaded, tears sliding down her cheeks. 'The Pendant. It's the Pendant.'

'Yes,' he hissed. 'The jade. It's perfect. Now just let me finish, let me complete my gift.'

'Stop it, Ranjit! You've . . . you've killed enough people

here already!'

'Yes of course, lest we forget, there was Jessica too.' He gave Jake's body a scornful kick. 'Dear Jessica.'

'No,' whispered Cassie.

'Yes,' he snarled, his red eyes burning into hers. 'I didn't suck her dry, of course. But I stayed away long enough to let the others do it. I let her down, I let her die. I'm good at that, Cassandra. I'm good at that. Like you told me. But now . . . Now I'm making it up to you, don't you see?'

She closed her eyes briefly, struggling for control.

'Did you hear me? Did you hear why she died screaming? It was me . . . but it was·him too!' This time it was Richard's ribs he kicked. 'Clever little Dick, chattering and delaying till Jessica was dead. Well, why not? She was only a mortal.' Ranjit laughed bitterly again.

'Ranjit, take the Pendant off!'

'Not on your life,' he grinned. 'Or his.'

He snatched at the air above Richard, and this time the boy's whole prone body floated up to him. Already it looked dry and empty, the veins staring, the life almost gone. How was he doing that . . . ? He couldn't be, could he?

But he was . . . He was projecting his spirit.

The Pendant was allowing him to draw out his

spirit, just as it had said in the manuscript. He could control it, *project* it, use its power just like Cassie could with Est—

No more talk, no more time. With a scream of fury Cassie lashed her own power at Ranjit again, this time with absolutely all of her newly fed strength. He was flung back, skidding on the floor, but he rolled and sprang up as if she'd barely grazed him.

'Don't make me do this, Cassie.' But he flew at her.

She felt his full weight slam into her, knocking her back, before he was anywhere near her. Before she could recover from the blow, he was next to her, his fist slamming into her gut, winding her. He seized her throat.

Recovering, struggling and roaring, she wrestled him off, striking out blindly with her projected power. Dimly she heard his gasps and shouts of pain as she beat him back, but then he was recovering and coming for her again. His fingers closed round her neck, and together they toppled backwards.

Let me in! He wants to separate us, he wants to kill me!

Estelle's screech was panic-stricken.

Cassandra! You'll die and I will too!

No way. No way . . .

SELFISH GIRL! He wants to SEPARATE US! Or KILL US!

Fighting two of them wasn't helping – especially as

Cassie couldn't help but feel the consuming, overwhelming passion even as they exchanged blows . . .

Ripping at his face with her fingernails, Cassie struck again and again at his head and his chest, but he was too strong. His fist caught her stomach again, and as she grunted and doubled up, he struck the side of her face, knocking her away. Before she could get back on her feet he was on top of her, gripping her hair, twisting her head back, rolling her on to her side and then her stomach. His knee was hard between her shoulder blades, holding her down as he gripped her head, and she knew through a film of pain that he was about to snap her neck. He might love her, but he was crazy. Insane. His twisted love wouldn't stop him killing her.

She went limp suddenly, so that he was thrown momentarily off balance, then she wriggled and kicked free, and slammed a foot into his chest. With a shout of anger, he fell back.

NOW! LET ME IN! LET ME BE WHOLE, THEN WE CAN DEFEAT HIM!

NO!

He sprang back up. They edged warily round the octagonal tomb, each eyeing the other, but Cassie's breath was coming in short gasps now, and he was cool, collected, his grin widening. She didn't have a lot left.

She'd have to be more precise.

KILL HIM! YOU HAVE TO KILL HIM OR WE'LL DIE!

Some change of heart since last term, Estelle, she managed to think – just as she realised, with horror, that the spirit's words were nonetheless true.

Summoning every last shred of her power, Cassie felt her face twist into a soundless snarl of implacable fury, and the force coalesced in her hands. Twisting them on thin air, she felt Ranjit's throat. And she squeezed.

He stumbled, went down on one knee, a look of shock in his bulging scarlet eyes. Grimly she let her hands fall to her sides, but she didn't let the force loosen on his neck. She had the focus now. Keep it. She had to keep it.

His beautiful face was purpling and swelling, his lips drawn back from his teeth as his fingers snatched at his throat. He grimaced in agony, sucked for air he couldn't get.

Tears stung her eyes, blurred her red vision, but she didn't let go.

Tighter. Harder. She focused the force, crushing his neck, not letting him gather himself enough to strike back. A horrible sound was coming from Ranjit's throat, and he was on both knees now, falling forward.

Something swung forward again, gleaming malevolently in the pale dawn. Writhing jade creatures, frantic now, squirming as if it was them she was choking.

With the last of his strength he twisted his face up to hers. It was full of hate, full of fury, full of thwarted blood-lust, but it was Ranjit's face.

Ranjit's.

Oh, *God*, what was she doing?

With a shriek she released his throat, but in the same motion she looped the disembodied force around the silver chain, yanking it hard. Ranjit gurgled as it jolted him sideways on to the stone floor.

He was beaten. Raising the Pendant with her power, dragging his head till it was once more twisted towards her, till she was hanging him on the thing, she gritted her teeth and snapped the chain.

Ranjit collapsed to the ground. But the Pendant flew clear, hitting the nearest sarcophagus, clattering on to the floor with its broken chain snaking round it.

And then there was silence.

CHAPTER TWENTY-SEVEN

Cassie began to shake, her hands at her mouth. She didn't dare look at any of the three unmoving bodies, so she stepped hesitantly closer to the jade Pendant.

It still glowed faintly, with a ghostly green light, but the creatures were frozen in place, motionless. Warily she stepped around it and next to the nearest sarcophagus. The surface of the jade looked so smooth and touchable; her fingers flexed towards it, but then she lifted her hand to her mouth and bit her knuckles.

'Cassie . . . ?'

She whirled around. The whisper was dazed and shaky. She saw Ranjit half sitting up, rubbing at his bruised neck. Her heart bounded, and she couldn't repress a cry of relief. She knew instantly. He was himself again. He was Ranjit again.

She fell to her knees beside him, weeping. 'I'm sorry,

I'm so sorry.'

'You had to . . . I . . . I didn't mean to . . .' He clutched at his head, shaking it, and whispered again, so low she had to lean close to him to hear. Little electric impulses sparked between his skin and hers. She leaned her face against his bleeding head, and put her arms around his trembling shoulders.

Whatever the circumstances, it felt good to touch him again.

'Oh, God.' He was barely audible, and he didn't respond to her touch. 'Cassie. What have I done?'

'It's OK. It's OK.'

'No. It isn't.'

She gulped. Somehow it hadn't occurred to her that he might remember it all, remember *everything* . . .

'I'm s-sorry,' he croaked. He tried to lift his head to look at Richard and Jake, but Cassie held him fiercely, not letting him see them.

'I'm telling you, it's OK. It was the Pendant. The Pendant, it was cursed, it made you . . .' She tailed off and kissed his hair, but he flinched away.

He drew a ragged breath, shaking his head violently. 'It couldn't have happened without me seeking it out, without me doing it. The m-murders. Somewhere deep inside, that must have been my idea. It must have come from me.'

She could think of nothing to say, so she hugged him harder. It was probably true. Him – and his spirit. It was strong, but it was dark. A personality clash, he'd once said.

A sound, drawing closer, hard to recognise at first. She turned towards it, craning her ears desperately. Was that a car? No, not a car. Could it be a speedboat, out on the quiet night-time Bosphorus? Yes. It was coming from the Academy's direction, the sound travelling across the otherwise still water; her senses still bristling with power, Cassie knew it for sure. It was still distant, but it was drawing in closer to the shore.

Ranjit must have heard it too. He went rigid in her arms, then sprang up, shaking her off.

'Who is it?'

'It must be Isabella. But she can't drive a boat, she told me that over the holidays. I bet she went to get Sir Alric.' She practically spat his name.

'Then I have to go.'

'Ranjit, wait!' She put her hands against his face. It was still pale, strained with disbelief, and his eyes, though not red any longer, were glazed with horror.

'Please, Cassie. I didn't mean for this to happen. Any of it!' Gripping her hands he drew them down from his face and kissed them. 'Tell him that!'

'Tell him yourself!' Despite everything, Cassie shivered at the touch of his lips. She leaned over quickly and kissed his face. 'Ranjit, Sir Alric will understand better than anybody. He'll know about the Pendant, he'll know what to do. He—'

'No! I can't stay here. I've k-killed—' He gasped in a breath as it hit him all over again. Staring at Richard and Jake, he backed away, shaking his head.

Cassie followed him, desperation sending prickling tears to her eyes. 'Please,' she whispered. She caught his hand. 'Please stay, and we'll fix it.'

Footsteps, running footsteps, and distant shouts. Ranjit looked up, panicked, then turned to her and caught her face between his hands again, staring into her eyes with ferocious love. 'That's what I wanted to do, fix it! I wanted to fix everything, make it better between us, that's all. If you weren't Few, if the spirit was gone, then we could be together, do you see?'

'Ranjit, how did you reckon it could do that?' She touched his cheekbones, the bridge of his nose, his lips. 'Sir Alric was the one who said we can't be together. You agreed. There's nothing else keeping us apart.'

'Yes, there is, and you know it. Our spirits, the conflict between them. *They're* what's keeping us apart. But Estelle's spirit, her not being fully joined with you, I thought . . . The Pendant, it can draw the spirit's power out; the Knife can divide the spirit from the host altogether; the Urn can contain it. I wanted to get her out of you!'

NO! Wicked boy, wicked boy—

Cassie shook her away. 'Heal wounds, break old ties. I know. I understand. See, you didn't mean to cause harm, you—'

'But I did.'

'But you always told me the spirit had a right to live. If you took her out of me, she could die, Ranjit!'

'I thought . . . oh, God knows what I thought. You know what? I didn't care. If Estelle's spirit died, so be it. I just wanted you back, Cassie! I wanted you free, like you wanted to be. You didn't choose this. I just . . . I just wanted you back!'

There were tears in Cassie's eyes again, and she couldn't reply.

He will harm ME! Kill him, kill him, kill him!

She didn't react to the spirit screaming in her head. It was too important to focus on him, keep him here, make him stay. 'Ranjit—'

'I have to go.'

'No,' said Cassie faintly. 'No . . .'

Abruptly, Ranjit drew her face to his, and kissed her on

the lips. Cassie wrapped her arms more fiercely around him, trying to hold him there. It was no good. He forced himself to pull away from her, and she saw there were tears in his eyes too.

'Stay,' she whispered.

'I love you, Cassie.'

And then he snatched up his bag, and vanished into the shadows.

CHAPTER TWENTY-EIGHT

The footsteps were on the stone steps of the portico now, Cassie could hear them. Two people, running. Shouting her name. Shouting Ranjit's. And *Jake's* . . . It was Isabella. Her guess had been right. Isabella and Sir Alric. Cassie felt a flash of furious rage at the Academy's head: this was all his fault. He could have stopped *everything*!

Quickly she turned to the Pendant once more. Pearly-green, it lay still, a toxic gleam against the ancient stones. Crouching, she reached for it, and as her fingers came closer she saw the creatures begin to stir. A fanged mermaid yawned, a coiling snake unravelled, a leopard stretched . . .

'DON'T TOUCH IT!'

She jerked round, stumbling upright. Sir Alric stood beneath the first arch, a leather briefcase in one hand, staring in horror at the scene. Behind him, Isabella shoved past, almost tripping in her haste to get to Jake. She fell to her knees beside him with a cry, as Sir Alric strode across to Richard and knelt beside him, touching the pulse at his throat. Cassie felt her own heart beating crazily.

'Somebody help, please!' screamed Isabella. 'Somebody help Jake!'

'Sir Alric, *please*,' Cassie urged him.

Sir Alric raised his head, and stared quite expressionlessly at Isabella and Jake. 'Quiet,' he snapped finally. 'In his turn,' he muttered to himself.

Opening the briefcase, Sir Alric drew out a familiar, delicately beautiful box, and a bog-standard disposable syringe. The Tears of the Few, realised Cassie, blinking in recognition.

Cassie crouched beside him as he ripped the syringe package with his teeth and pushed up Richard's sleeve. 'W-will they be OK?'

He didn't bother to answer, simply found a vein inside Richard's elbow and plunged in the syringe. He'd barely slipped it free when Richard sucked in a high breath and his eyes snapped open. Reflexively he jolted up, wobbled, and Cassie put her arms around him to stop him falling back hard to the floor.

'Richard?' she said urgently. 'Are you all right?

God, I'm sorry, I'm—'

'Bloody hell.' His voice came out on a shuddering breath. 'Another one, James, and make it a double.'

She gasped with relief, still clutching him close as she turned to Sir Alric. But his stare was cold granite.

'Where is he?'

Cassie knew who Darke meant. 'Gone,' she whispered.

'*Help me!*' screamed Isabella again.

Ignoring her, Sir Alric sucked in an angry breath. 'Why didn't you stop him?'

'How could I? Ranjit was distraught, he was crazy, I— Look, please, go and help Jake!'

He silenced her with a dismissive gesture. 'You know you could have kept him here, Cassie.' He gave her a cold look as he snapped on a pair of gloves. 'And you know that you should have done.'

Why the gloves now? He hadn't paused before he gave Richard the— Oh. Cassie watched dully as Sir Alric stooped down to the Pendant. The thin gloves, now that she looked properly, didn't seem like ordinary latex: they had a silken, watery sheen. Delicately Sir Alric lifted the Pendant by its chain and dropped it into the leather briefcase.

Then, standing up at last, he sighed, walked over, and crouched down opposite Isabella beside Jake. 'Please calm down,' he said. 'Don't be hysterical; that won't help him.' Sir Alric glanced up into the girl's white face for a moment, then very gently he slid the Knife from Jake's fingers. That too he dropped into the case, then he snapped it shut. Isabella watched him with frightened eyes.

'H-he's going to be OK, yes?' she said, her voice high with panic.

Sir Alric laid two fingers against Jake's neck, but Cassie had the distinct sense he was only going through the motions. He paused for what seemed like an age, as if he didn't want to meet Isabella's eyes. The only sound in the mausoleum was the Argentinian girl's terrified, echoing breathing.

Getting to his feet, Sir Alric left the briefcase sitting beside Jake and walked swiftly round his body to Isabella. Clasping her arm firmly he drew her up. She turned to him, wild-eyed.

'He'll be OK?'

'Cassie, come and help here,' he said, not answering.

'Let me go!' Isabella cried. 'Jake!'

'Cassie, I said come *here*!' snapped Sir Alric.

A switch tripped in Cassie's brain. Squeezing Richard's shoulders once more, she stood up and did as she was told, putting an arm round Isabella's waist. She felt frozen and distant. 'Isabella. Come on.'

'Cassie, what— No!' Isabella struggled as Cassie steered her away from Jake and pulled her towards the door. 'Let me go! Let me *go*!' She swore and kicked, lunging for Jake.

Cassie locked her arms tight round her friend, gritting her teeth, and grimaced at Sir Alric. 'What about Richard?'

'He's fine.' Sir Alric was flexing and stretching his gloved fingers, as if he too wanted to just snatch up the briefcase and leave. 'Now get Isabella out of here.'

Cassie nodded, and pulled Isabella with her as she backed out of the tomb. She thought the girl might get free – she was so scared of hurting her – but Isabella quite suddenly went limp in her arms. As Cassie pulled her out through the portico, she was weeping helplessly, unable to speak.

'Isabella? Oh, God, Isabella . . .' Cassie said, hugging her friend hard, and knowing all too well that her grip was all that was holding the girl up. Behind them, Cassie heard Richard staggering out through the archway, propping himself groggily against a pillar and catching his breath. She frowned at him, concerned.

'Can you manage?'

'I'm fine. Just about.' He sounded unusually empty, and

he was staring at nothing. 'Better than—' Catching Cassie's eye, he swallowed. 'Let's get out of here.'

'What did Sir Alric say?'

'He told me to go with you to the boat. Help you with Isabella.'

'What the hell's he doing?' exclaimed Cassie, eyes burning. She didn't want to hear Isabella's wrenching sobs any more but she couldn't let go of her.

'God knows. Cleaning up the evidence, probably. He was adamant we're to go.'

Cassie rubbed one sleeve across her face as Richard came to her side and kissed her cheek. He too put an arm round Isabella to support her. Dawn was a hazy pearl light now and beyond the mosque grounds the city was coming alive, car horns blaring, people shouting and laughing and calling out. Normal life, thought Cassie. Normal life. High on the air a recorded muezzin cried mournfully, amplified and rebounding off ancient stone and modern streets.

'All right.' Cassie's voice was hardly more than a whisper. She hugged Isabella tighter and led her towards the stone steps, though it was like moving some inanimate chess piece. 'We'll do as he says. For now. But not for ever.'

CHAPTER TWENTY-NINE

Perhaps he was never going to speak. And that would be fine. If Darke never spoke, maybe Cassie would never have to think about any of this. She'd just sit here till the end of time, on this richly upholstered Ottoman sofa, knees together and hands clasped tightly, while Sir Alric leaned against the arched stone window frame and stared out across the green garden and the sea to the dusky Istanbul skyline.

'I did a terrible thing when I brought Jake Johnson to this school.'

Oh well. The silence couldn't last for ever.

'It's too late to think that.' She ought to add something like *You couldn't have known* or *It wasn't your fault*. But she couldn't say anything like that. Not right now. She had absolutely no problem with sharing the guilt, especially with a man like Sir Alric Darke. He was more than equally

287

culpable. And if she felt the full weight of it all herself then she'd implode. Every time she closed her eyes she saw Jake's limp body, the terrible angle of it . . . the blood. Sometimes she thought she'd never sleep again.

She wanted to press Sir Alric for every detail about Jake, but somehow she couldn't bring herself to do it.

'How did you find out, Cassie? About the Pendant?'

She met his gaze. 'What do you mean? Richard called me, saying he and Ranjit were going to meet, but by the time I got to Hagia Sophia, Ranjit was crazy. I didn't know it had anything to do with the stupid Pendant.'

He didn't blink. He watched her eyes for a long and steady minute, but at last let it go. She was confident now that he believed she knew nothing about the artefacts' true nature.

'You should not have let Ranjit leave, Cassie.'

'Yeah, so you said.'

He turned, clearly irritated, but he couldn't look at her directly.

'He's had some sort of a breakdown. Anything might happen to him.'

'He's himself again, I told you.' And you, she thought, are still keeping things from me. Perhaps he always had.

'The boy has killed three people. Who knows what's going through his head right now?'

'That's why I would never have forced him back. Even if I could. He wasn't himself then. He felt guilty enough.' She sat back on the sofa, hugging herself, but not dropping her fierce gaze.

'Oh, you could have stopped him. I think we both know that. You've let your misguided loyalties get in the way of bringing Ranjit to justice.' He lowered himself into his desk chair, his angry gaze holding Cassie's. 'And in any case, why, Ms Bell, would Richard have gone to see Ranjit alone?'

'I don't know,' she lied. She knew at least part of the reason. He wanted to help Cassie, to prove his worth.

'It's an absolute mess.' Sir Alric's eyes held a faraway look now. Probably worried about answering to the Council, Cassie thought with no sympathy. 'Isabella was out of her mind, smuggling Jake into the school,' Darke continued. 'What did she hope to achieve?'

'I doubt she wanted to *achieve* anything. She loved him. She wanted to see him, she wanted to help him. What's so terrible about that?' she said, her jaw tense.

'Look how this has ended, Cassandra.'

'That's not Isabella's fault. Don't think you can dump our guilt on *her*.' Cassie stood up and walked to the bookshelf. She could still sense the Few manuscript, behind the old leather spines, hidden in its safe.

He gave a small sigh. 'How is Ms Caruso faring, in any case?'

'The doctor gave her sedatives. Her parents are coming to get her this afternoon.' There was nothing else to add. How was Isabella? She dreaded to think. As for what Sir Alric planned to tell the world about Jake's death: Cassie didn't care. That was his problem, and one he richly deserved. Let him try and cover it up again.

But there was someone she did still care about. 'Will Richard be OK?'

'Yes. Though it was a close call. Without the Tears, he would have died.'

'Yeah, I know,' she said wryly, remembering the injection she herself had received at the start of the previous term. 'Those Tears are strong stuff.'

'Astonishingly strong stuff,' he murmured.

Cassie eyed him closely. She was desperate to ask what he had done with the Knife, and the Pendant, but she held her tongue.

'In any case,' Sir Alric said, standing once more, 'I suggest you get back to classes, or people will begin to speculate on your absence.'

'Right. Because they're not talking already at all.'

He opened the door and stepped back. 'It will work out, Cassie.'

She walked past him without a backward glance. His promises meant as much as his version of truth. She felt his stare, and even some odd sense of his regret, but she didn't once turn back to look at him.

The Asian side of Istanbul looked almost close enough to touch. Drinking strong black coffee, Cassie and Richard sat silently, overawed by the view of the massive Rumelihisari Fort and the narrow blue neck of the Bosphorus.

'They used to call it "Throat-Cutter" when they built it,' remarked Richard, sitting back in his wooden chair and staring at the fort. 'Must've been impossible to get past it.'

'Seems appropriate.' Cassie smiled at him. He seemed strangely subdued, and in the mood for gloomy introspection. It wasn't like him, but it was understandable.

Still hungry, she glanced at Richard's untouched plate, and with a brief wink he slid it across the flowered tablecloth. Hesitating only for a moment, she shrugged and tucked into what was left of his white cheese, bread and olives. Breakfast at the breezy wooden café tasted like the best she'd ever eaten. It must be the fresh sea air, and the long taxi ride . . . and the narrow escape from death. Again.

For some of them, at least.

But she was trying not to think about Jake, and Isabella, just for the moment. She couldn't. If she did she'd go mad. Closing her eyes briefly, she inhaled the salty breeze. Guilt or no guilt, it was good to be alive.

'Thanks, Cassie.'

She stopped chewing. 'You don't have to keep saying it. Honestly.'

'Not for that. I mean, for not telling Sir Alric about the Jess thing.'

'How do you know I didn't?' she said, smiling a little.

Richard rested his elbows on the table. 'He had me into his office for a debrief yesterday afternoon. If he'd known about Jess, about me delaying Ranjit . . . I'd have been gone by this morning. Out on my ear. You know that.'

'Couldn't do it to you.' She shrugged, then added quietly, 'I've lost enough friends.'

'Well, thanks. Especially since I *deserve* to be out on my ear.'

Cassie dropped her chunk of bread on to the plate and clasped her hands. 'Richard . . . could you not have told me earlier? It would have explained such a lot.'

And, she didn't add, it might have helped her persuade Jake of Ranjit's innocence, long before any of this had happened. Things might have turned out differently. But

Richard must know that. She wouldn't rub it in.

'I've tried to tell you. Really. It was never the right moment.' He gave a rueful smile. 'When would it ever have been?'

'I know. I understand, I do. I just wish you'd trusted me enough to try and explain.'

'But I did try. Remember that night on the beach? I was this close to telling you. And then . . .'

She raked a hand through her hair, biting her lip hard. 'Oh God, of course. And then Yusuf's corpse washed up. Of course. I'm sorry.'

'And then in your room the other night, when we were looking at that printout? I tried again then but . . . we got distracted.'

She found herself blushing, remembering that impetuous kiss and the way it had made her feel.

Suddenly Richard looked alarmed. 'I didn't know, Cassie. I didn't *know* what Katerina was planning, or I'd *never* have been involved. You believe that, don't you?'

She met his eyes. 'Yes. I do, Richard.'

He bowed his head and rubbed his temples. 'I'll never forgive myself for that. Or for . . . for having put you in this position in the first place. I thought . . . I thought I was doing a good thing, getting you initiated, but—'

Reaching across the table, she placed her hand against

his cheek. 'It's OK, Richard. It wasn't you who killed Jess; it was Katerina and Keiko. And as for what happened with me. Well . . .' She sighed. 'It's water under the bridge now. It's OK.'

'It's not. But I'll have to live with it.' He gazed up at her, then placed his own hand over hers, holding her there.

'Richard.'

She should pull away now, she really should. It wasn't appropriate, it wasn't . . . a good idea. But she couldn't pull back, physically couldn't. It wasn't like the maniacal attraction between her and Ranjit, that impossible magnetism, not like that. But still she couldn't draw away. It felt too good. Too tempting.

Richard leaned across and as she watched his eyes, he licked his lips slowly and took a breath.

And then his mouth, warm and soft, was pressed against hers.

A sense of longing constricted her heart, combined with an electric thrill of lust. Almost involuntarily, her arm slipped around behind his neck, prolonging the kiss, his silky hair entwined into her fingers. She sought out his tongue, gave a small muffled gasp, and felt him pull her yearningly closer. But after a moment – a long, delicious moment – she drew reluctantly away. Her lips still tingled, but as she looked into Richard's eyes, it hit her once and for all that this wasn't really what she wanted. *He* wasn't really *who* she wanted. Guilt prickled at her conscience.

'Still too soon for me, buster,' she murmured. 'Too soon.'

To her surprise, he nodded. 'Yeah. I know.' His fingers were still curled around hers, and she didn't pull her hand away. A lock of his hair had fallen down over his right eye, and he was wearing that old roguish grin. 'Just registering my interest.'

Her breath caught at his directness. 'Cheeky.'

'And there was one other thing,' he said, his grin fading.

'Yeah?'

'I thought I should let you know that I love you.'

She burned her throat on her coffee. 'You what?'

'You heard.' He smiled at her expression before continuing. 'If you need me, Cassie, I'll be there. Right? But I promise you, no pressure. I don't expect anything other than friendship. And I'm sorry for everything I've done. But I'd spend a lifetime making it up to you.' He stood to go.

'Uh. Richard . . .'

'Yes?'

Well . . . ? Richard what? Cassie shut her eyes and

shook her head. That was two guys declaring their love in the space of a few days, and neither of them was a real possibility. One was on the run for murder, the other was . . .

The other wasn't Ranjit.

Cassie sighed deeply. She was on her own, whether she liked it or not. And she didn't. But that was life.

'Hey!' Richard interrupted, seeing her distress. 'Didn't I quite literally *just* say no pressure? I meant it, Cassie. And I mean the rest of it, too.'

Part of her wanted to throw herself into his arms, grab him and hang on to him, but Richard had already turned away and was walking out of the door, tossing a few bills to the café owner with a smile.

Getting her breath back, Cassie leaned on the table and stared out determinedly at the sea and the Asian shore. She wouldn't run after him. Though it would be so much simpler if she could . . .

No, no, my dear! Your first instinct was correct. Good gods, how could you even dream of—?

Cassie jerked straighter. Despite herself she had to muffle a chuckle. It was the injured bearing, the distinct tone of mortified pride.

'What's the problem, Estelle?' she murmured.

My dear! You know very well!

'No. Tell me.'

She could almost feel the spirit bristling. *We're strong, Cassie! We need only each other!*

Cassie didn't reply.

If someone wants to divide us, Cassie, we must be united against them. Against HIM. There's no room for yearning.

The morning sun on the water's surface was so blinding, Cassie had to shut her eyes against it. She didn't want to see anything, anyway. Didn't want to hear any more from Estelle, and certainly didn't want to think.

Ranjit.

Where was he? she wondered. Was he in hiding, miserable and guilt-ridden and scared? Or perhaps he'd recovered from the guilt, perhaps he was walking the streets, throwing caution to the wind, proud and disdainful, presenting a haughty face to the world and feeding where he liked? She shook her head. That seemed unlikely.

Was he thinking about her at all? Or had pure survival taken over?

It was good, at least, to know one thing for sure: she'd see him again. Of that she was certain. Had to be. She didn't know the circumstances, she didn't know if they'd be lovers, or killers, or both. Maybe they'd end up killing each *other*, once and for all . . .

Cassie opened her burning eyes, searching the bright morning Bosphorus for the hazy silhouette of the Academy.

For now Ranjit was lost, and so was their future. But she knew now, and there was no denying it to herself, that he was the one she wanted. Someday – maybe soon – she was going to find him again.

And then she would find their future, too. They'd be together, or it was all for nothing, everything they'd sacrificed. However brief, however deadly that time may be. She was certain now. They had to be together.

Sisters Red

'The wolf opened its long jaws,
rows of teeth stretching for her.
A thought locked itself in
Scarlett's mind: I am the only
one left to fight, so now, I must
kill you …'

An action-packed, paranormal
thriller in a gritty urban setting,
with a charming love story and
unexpected twist that leaves you
wanting more!

www.bookswithbite.co.uk

DARK HEART FOREVER

When Jane Jonas develops a friendship with an enigmatic stranger in town, it's exciting, it's new, and Jane wants him more than she's ever wanted anybody – until her mystery dream boy gets in the way.

Now Jane is caught between two worlds: one familiar, but tinged with romance and excitement; the other dark and dangerous, where angels, werewolves, and an irresistible stranger are trying to seduce her ...

THE SECRET CIRCLE

THE INITIATION AND THE CAPTIVE PART I

Cassie is not happy about moving from sunny California to gloomy New England. She longs for her old life, her old friends ... But when she starts to form a bond with a clique of terrifying but seductive teenagers at her new school, she thinks maybe she could fit in after all ...

Initiated into the Secret Circle, she is pulled along by the deadly and intoxicating thrill of this powerful and gifted coven. But then she falls in love, and has a daunting choice to make. She must resist temptation or risk dark forces to get what she wants.

THE SECRET CIRCLE

THE CAPTIVE PART II AND THE POWER

Now that Cassie is part of the most alluring and deadly clique imaginable, she is starting to realise that power comes with a price – more dangerous than she knows. Torn between the opposing desires of the two leaders of the Secret Circle, Cassie is struggling again. Does she use her considerable supernatural power to save lives, or does she put all her energy into keeping Adam, the boy she loves.

Cassie's relationship with Adam is threatening to tear the circle apart, so where does Cassie's loyalty and strength, truly lie?

NIGHT WORLD

Volume 2
Books 4-6
OUT NOW

Dark Angel

Angel saves Gillian from death in the icy wilderness and then offers to make her the most popular girl in school. But what does he want in return?

The Chosen

Vampire killer Rashel is torn between her feelings for her soulmate, Quinn, and her loathing for his thirst for human blood. She loves him, but is that enough?

Soulmate

Hannah's true love – Lord of the Night World, has come back into her life and reignited her passion. But her joy is threatened by the return of an ancient enemy ...

NIGHT WORLD

Volume 3
Books 7-9
OUT NOW

Huntress

In *Huntress,* Jez Redfern is leader of the Night World vampires,
yet she has an instinct to protect innocent mortals from her
former friends ... But can she resist her own desire for blood?

Black Dawn

In *Black Dawn*, Maggie's brother, Miles, goes missing. Her search
for him leads Maggie to the vampire, Delos. Whilst strangely
attracted to him she knows it's him or her brother.

Witchlight

In *Witchlight*, Keller is a shapeshifter. She is seaching for a new
Wild Power and battling her attraction to the dashing Galen. But
it seems he can never be her soulmate...

www.bookswithbite.co.uk

Sign up to the mailing list to find out about the latest releases from L.J. Smith

From the best-selling author of the Electra Brown series

RUNNING IN HEELS

From riches ... to bitches.

Daisy Davenport has it all — stunning looks, a spectacular house, a seriously gorgeous boyfriend.

But when her father is sent to jail for corruption, Daisy's life is shattered. Forced to move into rooms above a kebab shop, she and her family have to readjust — fast.

And if life isn't hard enough already, Daisy's new school is a world away from her old one. And the school bully is going to make sure she remembers it ...

FEB 2011

as hilarious as ever!

RUNNING IN HEELS

Helen Bailey

www.helenbaileybooks.com
www.hodderchildrens.co.uk